"So what would you like tonight to be?" Catherine asked.

Zack paused to consider. His eyes beamed a speculative challenge as he answered, "Whatever two strangers want to make of it."

"Without a tomorrow."

"Tomorrow I'm gone."

Well, that was laying it on the line! "Then I'll just take this one-night experience with the man behind the name," she countered, pride insisting that his schedule did not affect her expectations from this blind date, which had been zero before she met him anyway.

Sexual invitation simmered back at her. "I wonder if you will."

Emma Darcy

THE BLIND-DATE BRIDE

THE AUSTRALIANS

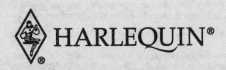

HARLEQUIN®

TORONTO • NEW YORK • LONDON
AMSTERDAM • PARIS • SYDNEY • HAMBURG
STOCKHOLM • ATHENS • TOKYO • MILAN • MADRID
PRAGUE • WARSAW • BUDAPEST • AUCKLAND

ISBN 0-373-12308-6

THE BLIND-DATE BRIDE

First North American Publication 2003.

Visit us at www.eHarlequin.com

Printed in U.S.A.

CHAPTER ONE

A BLIND Date...

Zack Freeman rolled his eyes at the idea of putting himself out for a woman he hadn't seen, knew nothing about, and would never meet again, given the work schedule he had lined up.

'She's a stunner,' his old friend, Pete Raynor, assured him.

'Stunners are two a penny in my world. All of them relentlessly ambitious.'

'That might be so in L.A., but this is home time in Australia, remember? Livvy's sister is something else.'

'Like what?'

His derisive tone earned a chiding shake of the head. 'You're jaded, mate. Which is why you're here spending a week with me. A night out with a gorgeous down-to-earth Aussie woman will do you good. Trust me on this.'

Zack winced at the argument, turning his gaze to the soothing view of the sea rolling its waves onto Forresters Beach. They were sitting on the balcony of a house Pete had recently acquired—his getaway from the pressure of being a dealer for an international bank. It was only an hour and a half away from Sydney, the perfect place to relax, he'd told Zack, persuading him into this week together, catching up on old times.

They'd been friends since school days and had always kept in touch, despite their different career paths. Pete was geared to competitive risk-taking while Zack had sought the creative fields opened up by computer technology. He'd built up a company that was now in hot demand for producing special effects for movies.

But he didn't want to think about work yet. Tomorrow he was booked on a Qantas flight to Los Angeles and he'd be getting his mind prepared for a series of important meetings, but today was still about recapturing the carefree days of their youth; eating hamburgers and French fries for lunch after a morning of riding the waves on surfboards and baking their bodies in the sun.

It had been a great week; not having to impress anyone or win anyone over. He and Pete had done all the things they used to do—playing chess, challenging each other to listen to their choice of music, drinking beer, swapping stories…just having fun.

He felt wonderfully lazy and didn't want to give up the feeling. Not until he absolutely had to. Here it was, Saturday afternoon Down Under, midsummer, and the living was easy. He didn't need a blind date. Didn't want one, either. His broad chest rose and fell in a contented sigh. This was more than good enough for him.

'Pete, I don't mind that you've got a date with your girlfriend. Go out and enjoy yourself. You don't have to look after me. I'll be perfectly happy with my own company.'

'It's our last night.'

Pete's unhappy frown pricked Zack's conscience.

'I can't get out of it. It's Livvy's birthday,' he went on, making it clear that Zack's refusal to go along with the plan put him into conflict.

The week had been special.

Was he being a spoilsport, ducking out on sharing this last night?

Livvy Trent, according to Pete, was very special. He'd met her walking her dog on this very beach. She even had a head for finance, holding quite a responsible position in the Treasury Department and living here on the central coast because she worked two days in Sydney and three in Newcastle. This could develop into a serious relationship, which was fine for Pete who was getting close to burn-out and looking for more from life than a tight focus on the world's money markets.

Zack was currently riding a high wave of success with a string of big movies featuring the special effects created by his company. No way was he ready to ease down from that creamy crest. He didn't have the time or the inclination to link up with a woman who wanted any kind of commitment from him. Too demanding. Too distracting. Besides, he was only thirty-three. He wanted what he had achieved. He wanted more of it. Finding *a special woman* could wait.

'I tell you, Zack, if I hadn't got to know Livvy first, I'd probably be chasing after her sister,' Pete ran on, intent on persuasion. 'Catherine is a knock-out.'

'So how come she's available on a Saturday night?' Zack dryly commented.

'Oh, same as you. Taking time out. Spending the weekend with her sister.'

'And I guess Livvy doesn't want to leave her alone, either.'

'No, she doesn't.' Realising he'd been tripped into the truth, Pete screwed his face into a hangdog appeal. 'So help me out here, will you, Zack? Please?'

He really cared for this woman. Zack hoped the feeling was returned and Pete wasn't being seen in terms of a good catch. Which he certainly was, financially. And he wasn't bad in the looks department, either. He was shorter than Zack but his physique was good, no flab on him.

His dark hair was receding at the temples and he'd had one of those ultra-short buzz cuts, defying the signs of encroaching baldness. Definitely a testosterone thing, Zack thought, but it had the advantage of never looking untidy, not like the wild mess of his black curls, although he figured they gave him an *artistic* image which was probably helpful in his business.

Pete had always had a very expressive face, not exactly handsome, but likeable. He had an infectious grin and his green eyes could quickly radiate a mischief that invited fun. Zack knew his own humour was more quirky, challenging to a lot of people, though Pete had always understood it.

Dark, he called it, often adding that Zack had to

have a dark and twisted soul to think up some of the special effects he created for movies. His olive skin tanned darkly, his eyes were dark, his teeth were very white—definitely a vampire in a previous life, Pete joked.

Whatever...on a surface basis, women were more drawn to him than they were to Pete. It was a fact of life outside of his control. He just hoped Livvy Trent would treat his friend right tonight—no roving eye.

'Okay. I'm in,' he conceded. 'As long as you accept that if I find this Catherine a total bore, I'll make an excuse to come home early.'

'Done!' Pete agreed, grinning his head off.

No problem in his mind.

Zack relaxed. Let tonight take care of itself, he thought, having dealt himself a ready bolthole.

A blind date...

Catherine Trent gave her sister a look designed to kill the idea on the spot. Stone dead. This weekend with Livvy was a much needed time out from *men*— one in particular—and even being polite to any male at the moment would be an effort she didn't want to make.

The look didn't work. It spurred Livvy into attack mode, eyes flashing the light of battle. 'You know your problem, Catherine? You've been fixated on Stuart Carstairs for so long, you've developed tunnel vision. Can't even see other men could be more attractive. And a lot better for you, too.'

So find me one, Catherine thought derisively, having done her own looking each time Stuart had strayed, then forgiving him and taking him back because there simply wasn't anyone else she wanted to be with. Compared to Stuart, other men were dull, but this last infidelity went beyond the bounds of acceptability. For him to snatch a bit of sex with a graphic artist in her own office, a woman who worked on the accounts she handled…that was too bitter a blow to her pride.

This had to be the end of their relationship. The final end. All the sexual charisma in the world didn't make up for a long, continuing string of hurts, especially this worst one, right under her nose. It was time to let go, time to move on, but to what?

'I'm not up to a blind date, Livvy,' she said flatly.

'Well, I'm not going to leave you here to mope alone,' came the belligerent retort.

'I won't mope. I'll watch videos.'

'Wallowing in escapism. I'll bet Stuart Carstairs isn't. Good old action man will be unzipping his trousers for…'

'Stop it!'

'No, I won't. He tried it on with me, too, you know. Your own sister.'

Shocked out of her irritation with Livvy's unwelcome nagging, Catherine shot a sharp look at her sister, unsure if she was speaking the truth or wanting to blacken Stuart's character beyond the pale. 'You never told me that before.'

A fierce conviction blazed back at her. 'I'm telling you now. Get rid of him. Get over him, Catherine. He might have the gift of the gab and he might be a great performer in bed, but he only ever thinks of himself. You're an ego trip for him. And every time you take him back you feed his ego more. Holding on to him is sick.'

Catherine frowned over these discomforting assertions. Was it sick to keep wanting a man who couldn't be trusted with other women? Stuart swore she was the only one who really counted in his life, but was that enough to hang on to? Obviously she couldn't count too much when he was hot for someone else, even her own sister.

'I won't hold on this time,' she muttered.

'Then let me see you take some positive action in another direction. Like partnering this other guy tonight,' Livvy strongly argued.

'I'm not in the mood.'

'You never are. Except for Stuart Carstairs who continually does the dirty on you. You've wasted four years on a dyed-in-the-wool philanderer and it's only ever going to be more of the same, him having it off with whomever he fancies, while you…'

'I told you it's over.'

'Until he soft soaps you again.'

'No. I mean it.'

'Fine! So you should be celebrating being free from him, giving yourself the chance to eye off someone else.'

She was just like her dog with a bone. Catherine looked down at the miniature fox terrier sitting by Livvy's feet and was grateful he wasn't yapping at her, too. She did need to be free of Stuart, but in her own mind and heart first. Plunging into dating would only throw up comparisons that would keep him painfully alive in her thoughts.

In fact, Livvy had just spoiled her attempt to forget him for a while. Here they were, seated on the balcony of her sister's apartment, overlooking the Brisbane Water at Gosford, idly watching the boats sailing out from the yacht club, feeling pleasantly replete from a fine lunch at Iguana Joe's, during which Livvy had raved about her wonderful new boyfriend, Peter Raynor. Why couldn't she just be happy with her own personal life instead of attacking Catherine's?

'This guy has been a friend of Pete's since school days. Now that tells you he values the people he likes. He's not a user and a dumper,' Livvy ran on, relentlessly intent on persuasion.

'Friendship between two men has no relevance whatsoever to how either of them view or treat women,' Catherine tersely commented, wanting an end to the argument.

'Right! So now you're cultivating a negative attitude. Not even giving people a chance. And I might add Pete treats me beautifully.'

'Lucky you! But I don't want to be stuck with a guy I don't know and might not like.'

'You like Pete. His friend should be at least an interesting person. The food at The Galley is always good. It's my birthday, and the best birthday present you could give me is to see you enjoying yourself without Stuart Carstairs.'

'I have been. With you. Before you started on this blind date kick,' Catherine snapped in exasperation.

'As for birthday gifts, I thought you liked the bracelet I bought you...'

'I do.'

'...and the lunch at the restaurant of your choice. Wasn't that birthday treat enough for you?'

Livvy's eloquent shrug was apologetic but it didn't stop her from turning the screws. 'I just hate going out and leaving you alone, knowing you're miserable. I won't be able to enjoy the evening with Pete if you don't come with me.'

Emotional blackmail.

But there was caring behind it, Catherine grudgingly conceded, and she didn't want to spoil any part of her younger sister's birthday. Livvy had always been a pet, her naturally happy nature making her a pleasure to be with. Their parents were away on an overseas trip, touring Canada this time, so it was up to Catherine to make up for their not being here, showering love on their younger daughter. She thought she'd done enough but...would it really hurt to make the effort of being pleasant to a stranger tonight?

'It would be such fun, dressing up together,' Livvy pressed.

'I didn't bring dress-up clothes with me,' Catherine remembered, not so much seeking an excuse but simply stating the truth.

'You can try mine on.' The eager offer was rushed out. 'In fact, I've got a little black number that would look fantastic on you. It's a jersey so it doesn't matter you're more curvy than me. It will stretch to fit.'

More curvy and taller. And their taste in clothes

was different. Which was why they'd never swapped or borrowed. But what she wore tonight was not an issue, Catherine decided, as long as she pleased Livvy.

Twenty-nine today. Her little sister…who had her life more in order than Catherine had managed in her thirty-one years. Still, Livvy's career in the public service carried minimal stress and steady promotion, given a reasonable level of performance. The advertising world was far more cut-throat and Catherine spent most of her working days living on the edge.

Different lives, different needs, different natures, different…even in looks.

Livvy's hair had been very blond in her childhood and she'd kept it blond with the help of a good hairdresser. She kept it short, too, its thick waves cleverly cut and styled to ripple attractively to just below her ears. Having inherited their father's Nordic blue eyes and skin that tanned to a lovely golden honey, she always looked sunny and vibrantly alive.

Dark and intense were the words more often attached to Catherine. Her hair was a very deep rich brown, as wavy as Livvy's but worn long. There never seemed to be time in her life for regular hairdresser appointments. Currently it fell to below her shoulder-blades. Luckily she only had to wash it for it to look reasonably good.

Her eyes were more amber than brown, like their mother's, but her eyebrows and lashes were almost black, giving them a dark look. The only feature she'd inherited from their father was height. She was a head taller than Livvy who had his colouring but their mother's more petite figure.

Different to each other but family nonetheless.

Close family.

And Catherine liked to see Livvy happy.

'Okay, I'll go with you. But I'm taking my own car so if Pete's friend is a total disaster I can come home by myself whenever I like.'

Sheer delight lit up Livvy's pretty face.

Yes, it was worth the effort, Catherine thought, and resigned herself to sharing an evening with a man who would probably bore her to death.

A blind date...

She looked down at the little black and white fox terrier, sleeping blissfully at Livvy's feet. He'd been called Luther after Martin Luther King who'd done all he could to integrate the black and white races in America.

Bringing people together.

Catherine smiled at the dog who'd certainly brought her sister and Pete together. Maybe she needed a dog in her life. It was surely a better means of meeting men than Livvy's current plot. Bound to provide more lasting and devoted company, too. A steadfast, uncomplicated love.

Yes.

She'd give up Stuart and buy herself a dog.

A much better solution to her problems than a blind date.

CHAPTER TWO

PETE insisted they set off at a quarter to eight, even though it was barely a ten-minute drive around the coast to the beach town of Terrigal where they were dining in style tonight. Livvy and Catherine were to meet them at the restaurant at eight, which probably meant anything up to an hour later. Zack had little faith in female punctuality, particularly with social evenings. Still, the less time he had to spend with his blind date, the better.

Terrigal was a prettier beach than Forresters with its row of Norfolk Pines lining the foreshore, but it was tame in comparison with none of the wild, dangerous surf that stirred the sense of primitive elements at play. This was a highly civilised beach; calm water, smooth sand, edged by lawns, a large resort hotel and many fashionable boutiques and restaurants. A yuppie place, not a getaway, Zack thought, glad that Pete had chosen to buy a house on an untamed shoreline.

The restaurant they were heading for was called The Galley, built above the sailing club on the other side of town and facing towards the Haven, a sheltered little bay where yachts rode at anchor. The main street traffic was heavy and slow. By the time they got through it and reached the parking area adjacent to The Galley, it was precisely eight o'clock.

Drinks at the bar coming up, Zack anticipated. He watched a zippy red convertible coming down the incline to the car park as Pete was collecting a celebratory bottle of Dom Perignon from the back seat of his beloved BMW. Had to be a Mazda MX-5, Zack decided, and was surprised to see two women occupying the open front seats. It was the kind of car guys would cruise in. Women were always worried about their hairstyles being blown awry.

'Told you they'd be on time,' Pete crowed, nodding to the car Zack was watching. 'That's Catherine driving.'

A long-haired brunette. The blonde in the passenger seat had to be Livvy. 'Is it her car?' he asked, finding himself interested by the unexpected.

'Yes. Livvy calls it Catherine's rebellion.'

'Against what?'

Pete shrugged. 'Being a woman, I guess.'

Zack rolled his eyes at him. 'You mean I'm about to be faced with a raging feminist.'

The answering grin was unrepentant. 'More a *femme fatale*. Just watch your knees. They might buckle any minute now.'

Not a chance, Zack thought.

She parked the convertible right at the end of the row of cars, the furthest point away from the entrance to the restaurant. Ensuring it wouldn't get boxed in, Zack decided, in case she wanted an easy getaway.

Which makes two of us, darling.

He and Pete waited at the BMW for the two women to join them. The black roof of the red convertible lifted from its slot at the back of the car and was locked in at the front. The blonde emerged first, waving excitedly at Pete. She looked very cute, wearing a clingy blue dress with shoestring shoulder straps. A pocket Venus for Pete, Zack thought, smiling at his choice.

Well, Catherine, strut your stuff, he silently challenged as a long rippling mane of very lustrous brown hair rose from the driver's side, the kind of hair that would look good on a pillow, Feel good, too. A tingle of temptation touched his fingertips. He clenched his hands to wipe it away. This was not the time to let a woman get to him. So she had great hair. The workings of the brain under it probably had no appeal at all.

She turned to close the door and lock the car. Zack's attention was galvanised. Pete hadn't lied. He hadn't even exaggerated. Catherine Trent was a stunner. Helen of Troy came to mind. Here was a face that could definitely launch a thousand ships. It seemed to simmer with sexual promise, aided by the erotic positioning of a deep pink flower over her right ear.

The tingle in his fingertips moved to his groin and there was nothing physical he could do to remove it. He tried willing it away. Impossible mission. She moved to the back of the car to join up with her sister and the full view of her was enough to blow any willpower right out of Zack's head. Even his side vision was affected. Livvy Trent blurred. Only Catherine remained in sharp focus.

She had a mesmerising hour-glass figure, mouth-wateringly lush femininity encased in a slinky little black dress with a short flirty skirt that barely reached mid-thigh on long shapely legs that Zack thought would feel fantastic wrapped around him. She was tall—tall enough to wear flat black shoes, though they looked like ballet slippers with straps crossed around her ankles. Somehow they were erotic, too, more so than kinky stiletto heels.

His gaze leapt back to her fascinating face as she came nearer. A slight dimple in her chin, a sultry full-lipped mouth, straight nose, angled cheekbones that highlighted the unusual shape of her eyes, more triangular than almond, amber irises, glinting golden between their black frame of thick lashes. Cat's eyes, he thought, but they didn't conjure up the image of some tame domestic cat, more an infinitely dangerous panther, capable of clawing him apart.

And why he should find that idea exciting he didn't know. Didn't think about it. It just was. He felt something dark and primitive stir inside him, wanting to take up the challenge she was beaming at him, wanting her submission to the desires she aroused, wanting to possess every part of her until he'd consumed the power she was exerting over him.

A *Class-A* hunk, Catherine thought when she first saw Pete's friend. Tall, dark and handsome with a body brimful of strong masculinity, his tight black jeans and the short-sleeved, open-necked white shirt showing off his impressive physique. Lots of surface sex appeal, but undoubtedly a bloated male ego to go with it.

'Wow!' Livvy murmured approvingly. 'Pete's friend sure measures up.'

Probably worked out at a gym in front of mirrors. Catherine was determinedly unimpressed, yet as they strolled towards the two men, a flutter started up in the pit of her stomach. It was the way he was looking at her, she argued to herself, assessing her female assets which, unfortunately, were on blatant display in Livvy's dress.

She hadn't cared earlier, even letting Livvy put the silly pink flower in her hair. It matched the spray of pink flowers featured on the black fabric of the dress, spreading diagonally from the left shoulder to the hem of the skirt. Livvy was into flowers in her hair this summer, using them as accessories to her outfits, but it wasn't Catherine's style. Not that it mattered tonight, except…she hoped Pete's friend wasn't seeing it as some flirtatious come-on.

On the other hand, if he wasn't too full of himself, he was certainly attractive enough to flirt with. Though that could be a dangerous play. She wasn't used to partnering a powerfully built man, and as she got closer, this man seemed to emanate power, the kind of big male dominant power that suddenly sent weak little quivers down her thighs.

Stuart was no taller than herself and his physique was on the lean side. His attraction lay more in a quicksilver charm than sheer physical impact. Catherine had always found eye contact and conversation sexier than actual bodies. All the same, she couldn't stop her eyes from feasting on this guy. He had an undeniable animal magnetism that tugged out a wanton wondering about what it might be like to have sex with him.

Different, she decided.

Not quite civilised.

Dark and intense.

Like his eyes…now that he was looking directly into hers.

Catherine sucked in a quick breath as her heart skipped into a wild canter. This guy had *it* in spades. With one searing look he burnt Stuart Carstairs right out of her mind and stamped his own image over the scar. It was a stunning impact. Catherine hadn't even begun to recover from it when she heard Pete Raynor start the introductions.

'Livvy…Catherine…this is my friend, Zack Freeman…'

Another stunning impact.

She *knew* him. Or rather, knew of him. Who didn't in the computer graphics business? Zack Freeman was already reaching legendary status for what he had achieved in special effects. He produced amazing stuff. And he was Pete's friend…her blind date?

Very white teeth flashed a winning smile. 'I'm delighted to meet you both. And I wish you a very happy birthday, Livvy.'

He offered his hand to her first—a perfunctory courtesy as Livvy thanked him—just a quick touch— then to Catherine, who found her hand captured by his for several seconds, making her extremely conscious of the warm flesh-to-flesh contact.

'I appreciate your giving me your company tonight, Catherine,' he said very personally, his voice pitched to a low, deep intimacy.

Her stomach flipped. She'd thought of Zack Freeman as some clever computer nerd with a weird creative genius, occupying some planet of his own. Yet here he was, right in front of her, so dynamically sexy she could scarcely breathe. It was a miracle she found the presence of mind to produce a reply.

'My pleasure.'

His smile was quite dazzling, given the dark tan of his skin. He had a strong nose, strong chin. His eyebrows were straight and low, his eyes deepset, somehow emphasising their penetrating power. His hair was a mass of tight, springy black curls which should have had a softening effect, but perversely added a sense of wound-up aggression.

'Nice car,' he said, nodding to where she'd parked. 'I like it.'

His eyes teased as he asked, 'What does it say about you?'

She already felt under attack from him and instinctively she fended off the probe that was asking her to reveal private feelings. 'Does it have to say anything?'

'Cars always say something about their owners.' He withdrew his hand and gestured to his friend. 'Now take Pete here. His BMW says he's made it. He's solid. He likes proven performance.'

'Right on,' Pete agreed.

'So what car do you own?' Catherine asked Zack, wanting to learn something about him.

He grinned. 'I don't. If I need a car, I hire one.'

'Don't let him fool you, Catherine,' Pete quickly inserted. 'Zack's a bikie from way back. He's got a whole stable of bikes to suit whatever mood he's in and whatever he wants to do.'

'An open road man,' she observed, thinking Zack Freeman had to have the kind of mind that would hate any form of confinement.

'Like you, Catherine,' Livvy popped in, all for encouraging this twosome.

Zack raised one eyebrow. 'True?'

She shrugged. 'I've only ever thought of my car as a somewhat impractical self-indulgence.' She shot a rueful look at her sister. 'Livvy's the one who analyses everything to death.'

'And I love her great sense of logic,' Pete said with relish, beaming pleasure in her sister. He held out the bottle he was carrying. 'Brought the best French bubbly to celebrate your birthday, Livvy.'

'Great!' She grabbed his arm, hugging it as he turned to lead them into the restaurant. 'I just love your sense of occasion, Pete.'

They were so obviously happy with each other, Catherine shook her head over the pressure exerted on her to make up a foursome. She eyed Zack Freeman curiously, aware that he could probably snap his fingers and pick up any woman. So why had he agreed to a blind date?

She remembered Livvy's argument, centred mostly on getting Catherine to rid herself of Stuart and open up to other men. Embarrassment squirmed through her at the thought that Livvy had engaged Pete's help to *fix up* her sister and she was some kind of charity case to Zack Freeman—doing a favour asked of him by his old friend.

A horrible sense of humiliation forced her to blurt out, 'Did Pete coerce you into partnering me tonight?'

He was slow to reply, possibly picking up her inner tension and musing over its cause. 'I had no other plans. Pete wanted me to make up a party of four tonight and I agreed.' His mouth quirked. 'No regrets so far. But if you have a problem with the arrangement…'

'No,' she rushed out on a wave of intense relief. He hadn't been told anything *personal* about her.

His head tilted quizzically. 'You want to cut and run?'

Truth spilled out before she could stop it. 'Livvy would kill me if I did.'

'Ah! So she coerced you.'

Catherine took a deep breath, wanting to get onto some kind of equal footing with him. 'It was more her idea than mine.'

'Does that mean you're anticipating pain with me?'

A nervous gurgle of laughter bubbled out. 'Let me fantasise pleasure for a while.'

'Good idea!' His eyes twinkled wicked mischief. 'I'll do the same.'

He half turned, waving her to fall into step with him to follow Pete and Livvy. He made no attempt to take her arm or hand, for which she was grateful since she was super-conscious of his physicality as it was, and any contact would feel sexual after her blunder in linking pleasure and fantasy.

'Livvy said you and Pete have been friends since school days,' she remarked, trying to dampen the sizzle she'd unwittingly raised.

'Mmm...going on twenty years. We're still the same people to each other. You get to value that as you move through life.'

'I guess you do a lot of role-playing with your work.'

He paused, slanting her a sharp look beneath lowered brows. 'You know what I do?'

Would he have preferred her not to know? To pretend he was just some regular guy for the night? Was he sick of women climbing all over him for what he was?

'It's okay. I won't blab on about it,' she assured him. 'I don't think Livvy knows. I happen to work with graphic artists who are interested in everything you come up with—big discussions—so when Pete introduced you...'

'You're a graphic artist yourself?' he cut in, an angry tension emanating from him.

'No. And I'm not a user, either,' she asserted, resenting the implied assumption that she might angle some benefit out of this meeting with him. 'You're perfectly safe with me, Zack Freeman.'

He gave her a long hard look that bristled with suspicion and she stared right back with fierce pride, finally earning a glint of respect.

'Oh, I wouldn't go that far,' he drawled, his mouth taking on a wry twist. 'You pack quite a punch, Catherine Trent.'

Heat whooshed up her neck and into her cheeks

as sexual electricity crackled from him and zipped into her bloodstream. Catherine was appalled at herself. She never blushed. She might flush in anger, but blushing belonged to adolescence and she was way past that. A sophisticated career woman did not blush.

'You're not exactly harmless yourself,' she retorted defensively, only realising it was an admission of the attraction he exerted after she had spoken. Not that it mattered. He knew anyway. Impossible for him not to be aware of his effect on women, just as she was aware that many men fancied her.

He shrugged. 'Sorry if I gave offence. This is my week off from being *the* Zack Freeman. In fact, it's my last night off. I have to go back to being him tomorrow.'

'You don't like being *him?*' Was being so successful such a burden?

'It has its rewards and I'm not about to give them up,' he stated, determination glinting in his eyes. 'But there's a time and place for everything.'

And it was clear he wouldn't enjoy being with some star-struck woman who raved on about what he'd achieved or tried to ferret out the key to his meteoric rise to fame in his field.

'So what would you like tonight to be?' Catherine asked, somewhat bemused by his wish to set aside the recognition that most men's egos would demand.

He paused to consider. His eyes beamed a speculative challenge as he answered, 'Whatever two strangers want to make of it.'

'Without a tomorrow.'

'Tomorrow I'm gone.'

Well, that was laying it on the line. No future with Zack Freeman. Not that she had had time to even think of one or consider whether it might be desirable.

'Then I'll just take this one night experience with the man behind the name,' she countered, pride insisting that his schedule did not affect her expectations from this blind date, which had been zero before she met him anyway.

Sexual invitation simmered back at her. 'I wonder if you will.'

She hadn't meant a *one-night stand.* Another wretched blush goaded her into being uncharacteristically provocative. 'You win some. You lose some.' It was a warning not to assume anything.

He grinned. 'The game is afoot. And you can't cut and run because your sister is watching and she'll kill you if you do.'

She laughed, trying to lighten the effect of a charge of nervous excitement. 'You think I'm trapped?'

'Why did you come?'

'To please Livvy. It's her birthday.'

'Then you have a giving nature. That's a trap in itself, Catherine.'

'Oh, the giving only goes so far.'

'What would you take, given the chance?'

'That's a big question.'

'And you don't intend to answer it yet.'

'That would spoil the game.'

He laughed, entirely relaxed now and enjoying the

flirtation he'd fired up and was stoking with every look and word. 'I guess we'd better join Livvy and Pete. They're waiting for us on the steps.'

So they were, paused halfway up the flight of steps to the restaurant and viewing her and Zack with an air of smug satisfaction—the successful matchmakers congratulating themselves on getting it right!

Except this blind date wasn't going beyond whatever happened tonight.

Remember that, Catherine sternly told herself as she walked beside the man who had every nerve in her body agitated, her heart thumping, her mind bombarded with tempting fantasies.

There is no tomorrow, she recited, meaning it as a sobering caution to be sensible. Yet somehow it had the perverse effect of inciting a sense of wild recklessness—a desire to *take* what she could of Zack Freeman while she could. To *have* him. All he'd give her. If only for one night.

CHAPTER THREE

SHE had ordered the three scoops of different ice-creams for dessert and was tasting them each in turn, sliding the loaded spoon between her lips, consciously testing the flavour on her tongue. Zack found the action so sensual, his whole body was tightening up. Catherine Trent was one hell of a sexy woman and the urge to race her off into the night and ravage her from head to toe had a powerful grip on him.

He wrenched his gaze away from her mouth and turned it out to sea. Their table was on the open veranda that ran the length of the restaurant and he'd taken refuge in the view several times tonight, needing to cool the desire that kept plaguing him. Was she as hot for him as he was for her? Would she go for it, given the limitation he'd stipulated?

One night…

Problem was, he might end up wanting more and that would mess him up. She was like a fever in his blood and he needed a cool head once he hit Los Angeles. It was the wrong time to meet a woman like Catherine Trent. She appealed to him on too many levels. He liked the way her mind worked, liked talking with her, liked having her across the table from him, watching her face, the expressions in her fascinating eyes, her body language.

She wasn't a stranger anymore, though he'd deliberately refrained from asking about her life, keeping their dinner conversation to very general topics. She'd still got to him, more than he recalled any other woman ever doing.

Better to let her go, he told himself. What had she said...*win some, lose some?* He'd never liked losing, but he had a lot at stake right now. Winning what he planned to win in L.A. was more important than losing out on a night of sex which could get him too involved with this woman.

'Do you think a full moon really does affect people?'

There was a full moon tonight, big and white, hanging in the sky where he had turned his gaze, but he hadn't been looking at it. Catherine's question drew an instant reply from Livvy who'd been bubbling with high spirits all evening.

'Course it does. The word, *lunatic* didn't evolve from nothing.'

'Historically it is associated with madness. And romance,' Pete chimed in.

'Which could be considered a form of madness,' Zack observed dryly, looking back at Catherine, hoping she wasn't nursing romantic thoughts about him.

It simply wasn't on.

Yet the pull of her attraction was very strong.

'I was just wondering...' The musing little smile on her lips had his gut contracting with the desire to kiss her. '...how connected are we to the physical world? We get irritated when it's windy. Sunshine tends to make us smile. The moon regulates the tides, so when it's at full strength like this, does it tug at things in us, too?'

Was she wanting an explanation for what she felt with him?

An excuse for it?

Something outside herself so she couldn't be blamed for wanting what he wanted, too?

'You mean like amplifying the feelings we have,' Livvy said speculatively. 'Making mad people even madder.'

'Swelling the tides of passion,' Pete rolled out, relishing that idea and proceeding to banter with Livvy about possible lunar effects on human behaviour.

'Don't forget animals,' Zack inserted after a while. 'Why do wolves howl at a full moon?'

'Because they prefer dark nights?' Catherine suggested, looking at him with her head on a tilt as though mentally likening him to a wolf who prowled dark places.

'Or maybe it's part of the mating game,' he couldn't resist saying.

Her thick lashes lowered, veiling the expression in her eyes, though not before he glimpsed a vulnerability to the mating they could share.

Temptation bit into his resolution to let her go.

She wanted him. He wanted her. Where was the harm in a one-night stand? It wasn't as though she was an inexperienced woman. Late twenties, he guessed, and given her face and figure, had probably been fending off or taking on guys since her mid-teens.

Her long throat moved in a convulsive little swallow. Dry-mouthed from the heat coursing through her? The low V-neckline of her dress pointed into the valley between her breasts, shadowed by the soft swell of lush feminine flesh on either side. He wanted to fill his hands with her, wanted to…

'Coffee, anyone?'

The waiter deftly removed the emptied dessert plates as choices were made around the table.

'Short black,' Catherine said,

Strong and dark, Zack thought, which was how he wanted it, too. 'The same for me.'

He didn't hear what the others ordered. The waiter departed. Pete suggested they walk on down the hill to the Crowne Plaza after they'd finished their coffee, disco the rest of the night away. Livvy applauded the idea. Catherine smiled at her sister but said nothing, waiting for Zack's reaction with no persuasion from her either way.

Hours of ear-blasting music and hot, sweaty dancing didn't appeal to Zack. Nor did a long sexual tease with Catherine that promised without delivering. She had burned him enough tonight. If there was to be any action between them, it was now or never, he decided.

Her choice.

'I hope you'll all excuse me—you, particularly, Catherine…' He offered her a rueful smile. 'I wasn't planning on a late night tonight. I have a car calling at seven-thirty in the morning to take me to the airport. I've enjoyed the evening very much but…'

'You don't want to be a total wreck tomorrow,'

she finished for him, smiling her understanding and with more than a hint of relief in her eyes.

Off the hook?

'I won't cut into your plan of action, Pete,' he directed to his old friend. 'I can call a taxi from here and the three of you can…'

'No need for a taxi,' Catherine cut in. 'I can drive you back to Forresters Beach on my way home.'

Excitement zipped through his veins. Opportunity had just been opened up. Was it deliberate, decisive, or merely flirting with a chance she might take? 'Thank you,' he said, anticipation surging into a storm of desire at the thought of being alone with her.

She looked at her sister. 'That's okay with you, isn't it, Livvy? Pete will bring you home after the disco?'

'Absolutely,' Pete agreed, happy to have Livvy to himself.

Her sister heaved a sigh and looked from Catherine to Zack, clearly exasperated by this abrupt end to their foursome. It wasn't what *she'd* planned but the decision had already been taken out of her hands.

Zack smiled at her. 'May I say it's been a delight to meet you, Livvy. You and Pete have yourself a ball tonight.'

'Hey! And wake me for a coffee with you before you leave in the morning, Zack,' Pete demanded.

'Will do.'

'You don't have to go home this early, Catherine,' Livvy pressed, frowning at her sister. 'It will only take ten minutes to drop Zack off at Forresters Beach...'

'I don't want you watching out for me at a disco,' she stated firmly. 'You and Pete should feel free to have fun together. It's your birthday.'

And that might be the straight truth of it, Zack cautioned himself. Being at a disco without a partner, guys on a high trying to pick her up...he could well imagine a fight breaking out over Catherine Trent...and that could be extremely tiresome if she wasn't in the mood to play. With anyone else but him.

Conviction fizzed through his mind. She need not have made the offer to drive him home. She could have waited until he'd left in a taxi, then made the decision not to go to the disco. This was not a safe play. The chance was on.

Catherine beamed her sister a flinty look that said enough was enough and there'd be no forcing her to circulate in a crowded disco where she might or might not hit it off with some guy. Impossible anyway after being with Zack Freeman all evening. Though her impulsive offer to drive him to Pete's place now had her stomach churning.

The move protected her from being thrown at more men, which Livvy had obviously intended once Zack removed himself from the field of play. It also protected her from any argument over her decision to leave since giving her blind date a lift home was a perfectly reasonable and polite thing to do in return for his company tonight. But it did mean she'd be

alone with him in her car and when they reached
Forresters Beach.

Would she be safe with him?

Did she want to be safe with him?

Livvy's resigned grimace set her free to do whatever she liked and Pete was obviously not troubled
by their party being cut in half. He'd done what had
been requested of him, supplying Zack for Livvy's
sister, and if the two of them went off together, that
was fine by him. He had the woman he wanted still
at his side.

The coffee arrived.

She hoped its hot bitterness would sober her up.
Not from alcohol. She'd only drunk one glass of
champagne. It was Zack Freeman's affect on her that
needed diluting down to something manageable. He
was like a magnet, playing a tug-of-war with every
female hormone in her body. Never in her life had
she been made to feel so aware of her own sexuality,
as well as a chaotic craving to experience his.

He had the most sinfully sexy eyes, teasing, challenging, flirting, knowing and constantly evaluating
the response he drew from her. He made her laugh.
He made her smile. He made her tingle all over. He
was the intoxicant and not even the knowledge that
he'd be gone tomorrow lessened the addictive power
of his attraction.

'So I get to have a ride in your car.'

She stopped sipping the coffee and looked up to
answer him, her heart squeezing tight at the warm
pleasure in his eyes. 'A short ride,' she said, reminding herself again of the brevity of this encounter.

One night...which was fast coming to an end.

'An impractical self-indulgence,' he drawled softly.

For a stomach-clenching moment, she thought he was referring to her decision to ride with him, whatever that might lead to between them. Then she realised he was repeating her own words about owning such a car.

'You get wet if it rains before you can stop to get the hood on,' she explained with a shrug.

'But you don't mind the wind in your hair.'

She smiled. 'Nor the sun on my face.'

'You like the feel of nature.'

'Yes.'

He smiled. 'An elemental woman.'

He made it sound intensely sensual, made her feel intensely sensual. She took refuge in sipping coffee again, trying not to wonder just how elemental he was and how he would look as nature had fashioned him.

The open-necked shirt had been tantalising her all throughout dinner, giving her a glimpse of tight black curls arrowing down his chest. His forearms weren't hairy, their darkly tanned skin gleaming like oiled teak. She imagined his whole body would be mainly like that with a sprinkle of black springy curls in the most masculine places. The desire to know, to touch, conflicted terribly with the sensible course of simply wishing him well and waving him goodbye.

He wasn't going to be in her life.

Except for this one night.

Pete paid the restaurant bill, insisting it was his

party treat for Livvy. Everyone had drunk their coffee. It was time to go. Nervous tension gripped Catherine as Zack moved to hold her chair back for an easy rise from the table. She looked at the full moon as she stood up. Was this *lust* for him a madness that she would shake her head over tomorrow?

She didn't understand it.

Was she raw and needful from Stuart's most recent dalliance with another woman? But she wasn't feeling any bitter hurt right now. It was as though all that was in a far distant place. Zack Freeman generated a physical immediacy that completely clouded anything else.

She was super aware of her legs moving in step with his as they followed Pete and Livvy out of the restaurant, aware that the top of her head was level with his chin, aware of the strength of the man and the weak little quivers running down her thighs, aware of her breasts straining against the stretch fabric of Livvy's dress, aware of the flutters in her stomach where the yearning to experience Zack Freeman was strong and deep and beyond any mental control.

Pete decided to drive down to The Crowne Plaza and have his car parked at the hotel for an easy pickup when he and Livvy had had enough of the disco. They said their goodnights at his BMW and Catherine and Zack watched them drive off before moving on to the end of the car park where her red convertible was waiting for them.

'Do you like to dance?' Zack asked as they strolled along.

He wasn't touching her, merely walking beside

her, but Catherine barely found breath enough to answer, 'Yes.'

'I'm sorry if you feel you're missing out.'

She shook her head.

'For me it would have been more of a torture than a pleasure.'

The wry statement drew her into glancing at him.

His eyes caught hers and delivered their own searing meaning as he elaborated. 'I would have wanted more than the touching permissable on a public dance floor, Catherine.'

She wrenched her gaze from his as heat whooshed through her entire body. The direct acknowledgment of the desire he was feeling for her left no way of dismissing it as possible fantasy. It was real. And it was vibrantly alive, pulsing through her, arousing eager responses that clamoured for expression.

Her mind tried to over-ride them. She didn't *do* one-night stands. She believed that casual sex diminished what should be really special to a relationship that shared far more than just sex. Men were different, she'd told herself, having excused Stuart's infidelities as meaningless rushes of testosterone. But she'd never felt so sexually *connected* to a man before, not even with Stuart at his charismatic best.

She fumbled in her evening bag for the car keys. Just a short ride and this…this raging temptation…would be over. Unlock the car, get in and drive Zack Freeman to Forresters Beach. He would fly away tomorrow and she'd come down to earth with a big thump if she strayed from what she believed in tonight.

But what if she never felt like this again?

Was she passing up a once-in-a-lifetime experience?

Would she always wonder?

Her fingers found the car key, curled around it, brought it out. Her hand trembled as she pointed the key at her car and pressed the remote control button to unlock the doors. Zack accompanied her to the driver's side, intent on doing the courtesy of seeing her settled on her seat. She waited by the door for him to reach out and open it. He stepped forward, then turned to face her instead.

'Have I embarrassed you?'

His eyes scanned hers with probing intensity, driving her out of her tongue-tied state.

'No.' She tried to smile but her mouth felt as wobbly as the rest of her. 'I think the wolf in you was howling just then.'

'And you didn't want to answer?'

'Wolves tend to keep to their own territory.'

'They have been known to cross boundaries if the call is strong enough.'

He reached up and touched the silk flower in her hair.

'It's not real.' Her voice emerged as a husky whisper.

'No. But this is, Catherine.' His fingers feathered her earlobe before sliding under the fall of her hair to the nape of her neck. 'This is,' he repeated, his voice a low erotic burr as he moved closer and bent his head to hers.

The drumming of her heart filled her ears, block-

ing out any last second denial her mind might have
dictated. A light tug of her hair tilted her face up.
She was beyond fighting this moment which shim-
mered with the promise of answers she craved. His
lips brushed hers, stirring a host of electric tingles.
Then came the tasting, a feast of sensual pleasure
that was more seductive than any kissing Catherine
remembered.

Her arms lifted and wound around his neck, her
own hands thrusting into his hair, fingers driving
through the thick mat of curls, pressing for a contin-
uation, wanting to know and feel more. He scooped
her body firmly against his and the hard, heated
strength of him was imprinted on her, the muscular
wall of his chest, rock-hard thighs, and an erection
that instantly set a wave of desire rolling through her,
inciting a wild, questing passion for satisfaction
when his mouth invaded hers. Long, fierce, ravishing
kisses…kisses in her hair, on her throat, shoulders,
her breasts yearning to be touched, taken, her stomach revelling in the feel of his urgent wanting.

A burst of laughter jolted them both out of the wild
compulsion to pursue more and more sensation. It
came from another group of people emerging from
the restaurant and heading for their cars. Zack sucked
in a deep breath, one hand lifting to cup her cheek,
fingers stroking soft reassurance.

'I know a private place. I'll drive us there.'

Her mind was too shattered to think. With quick,
purposeful strides, he bundled her around to the passenger side, all his energy focused now on taking her
with him. Catherine was still too tremulous to take

any positive action herself. He'd already guided her into the car and fastened her seat belt before she remembered...

'The key...' It wasn't in her hand anymore. 'I must have dropped it.'

'I'll find it.'

He bent and kissed her, stoking the need that had been left hanging. She sat dazed by the whole tumultuous eruption of passion. It didn't even occur to her that she hadn't given him permission to take control of her car. He settled behind the driving wheel, flashed her a dazzling grin as he fastened his seat belt, switched on the engine, and they were off.

'Where are we going?' she finally found wits enough to ask.

Another white grin—the grin of a man on a winning streak that couldn't be stopped. 'To a place that was made for us, Catherine Trent...a place that will give us a night to remember.'

CHAPTER FOUR

A NIGHT to remember... The seductive words kept
floating through Catherine's mind as Zack drove
through Terrigal, crossed the bridge over the lagoon,
and headed along Ocean Drive Road—all familiar
territory to her, yet nothing felt familiar on this jour-
ney with Zack Freeman.

They hadn't put the hood of the convertible down.
She was closed in with him and he seemed to dom-
inate the space inside the car, emanating an irresistible power that would pull her along with him
wherever he wanted to take her. That was seductive,
too, removing from her all responsibility for what
happened. Except Catherine knew that wasn't true.

She could still say no, though her gaze was continually drawn to the hands firmly wrapped around
the driving wheel, hands in control, sure of what they
were doing, and the wanton desire to feel those hands
on her clouded any decision. So far he hadn't done
anything she hadn't secretly yearned for. Why stop
now? Yet wasn't it risky, even dangerous, trusting
herself to him like this?

At the Wamberal roundabout he took the road that
led towards Forresters Beach. Catherine told herself
it would be easy to stop this madness now, insist he
drive to Pete's place and say she didn't want to take
this night any further. It was the safe thing to do, just

open her mouth...and lose out on having Zack
Freeman as her lover for one night.

This immensely desirable man...

Even in profile he was strikingly handsome. And
his aggressively male physique had a sexual power
which stirred basic instincts she could neither ignore
nor deny. More than that, every time he looked at
her, his eyes seemed to connect to what she was
thinking, what she was feeling...dark burning eyes,
challenging her to acknowledge that the desire between them was *real*. Not a fantasy. Real and urgent
and compelling. Every jangling nerve end in her
body was still affirming this reality.

Whether it was right or wrong for her...was such
a question relevant at this point?

She was over thirty. *Thirty-one*. And going no-
where with the man who'd monopolised her interest
for the past few years. It was time to face the fact
that Stuart Carstairs was a footloose philanderer and
always would be. Zack Freeman might be one, too,
for all she knew, but at least he wasn't pretending to
have fallen in love with her and he'd been honest
about not holding out more than one night with him.
This blind date did not have a blind end to it. She
knew precisely what was on offer.

Well, not precisely. Her imagination was running
riot, fueled by the feelings Zack had stirred in her.
It might be a wild, reckless act to ride this tide until
time ran out but she didn't want to go home wondering what it might have been like. She *needed* to
know there was something more than Stuart had

given her, something she could look for in the future, knowing it was *real*.

The car slowed, turned into Crystal Street, the road to Pete's place. 'We're going to Forresters?' she blurted out, seized by the panicky thought that *he* had changed his mind, deciding she wasn't worth losing sleep over.

'No.' He flashed her a smile that sparkled with anticipation. 'To a little bay just past the headland at Forresters. You'll see. It's the perfect place for us.'

Perfect... He didn't have any doubts. There was no struggle over any sense of right or wrong in his conscience. It was full steam ahead for Zack Freeman. And maybe that was part of his strength, part of his overwhelming attraction. He knew what he wanted and went after it with single-minded purpose.

They turned right at the end of Crystal Street. The car climbed a steep hill—the headland—went over it and down the other side, turning sharp left and coming to a halt in a large dead-end parking circle that was closed in by a nature reserve, a thick belt of trees and bushes cutting off any sight of the ocean.

Shadows from overhanging foliage put them in a pool of darkness. There were no other vehicles here. The sense of being very much alone with Zack Freeman sent a quiver of apprehension down Catherine's spine. Was she mad to do this? Was she?

Then he was opening the passenger door, drawing her out of the car and into an embrace that shot a flood of positive responses through her body, swamping any chilling fears. He planted soft little kisses around her face, gentle smiling kisses, transmitting a pleasure in her that Catherine revelled in.

'Do you have a rug in the boot of the car?' he murmured.

She always kept a picnic rug there. More a rubber-backed mat than a rug. It could be laid on damp ground. Or firm, wave-washed sand. She could hear the ocean now, booming behind the trees, and the idea of a secluded little beach all to themselves misted what they'd be using the rug for in a romantic haze.

'Yes,' she said, and knew it was a *yes* to all that might ensue, regardless of how reckless it was.

Again he cupped her cheek, subjecting her eyes to an intense focus from his. 'I didn't come prepared for this. Tell me now, Catherine, do I need to use...'

'No. There's no risk. Unless...' Did he have sex indiscriminately, whenever and wherever the urge took him?

He read her question and shook his head. 'I've always been careful.' His mouth tilted ruefully. 'You're the only woman who's made me forget...momentarily...what intimacy can lead to.'

The power of his desire for her was exhilarating. The only woman... And he was the only man who had ever incited this compelling sense of need in her. A man of control, she thought giddily, a man she could trust to look after her.

He collected the picnic rug from the boot of the car, then took her hand, holding it with warm possessive strength as he led her onto a paved path that wound through the nature reserve. It stopped where the beach began. With the shadows of the bushland behind them and the full moon lighting their way, it was easy to see the boards marking sand-filled steps which took them down a long dune to the seashore.

'Sit for a minute,' Zack commanded, pausing to drop the rug on the step behind them. 'I'll take your shoes off.'

The first bit of undressing, Catherine thought, her heart thumping erratically as she sank onto the rug-covered step and Zack descended a couple more before crouching to remove her shoes. She hadn't worn stockings or pantihose. It was a hot night. It felt even hotter as Zack handled her ankles, undoing the criss-cross straps, his fingers sliding along the soles of her feet with each shoe removal, making her toes twitch from the sensitivity aroused by his touch.

'Cramp?' he asked.

'No. Just...'

He massaged her toes anyway, leaving her speech-less and breathless.

It was some slight relief when he handed over her shoes and sat down beside her to take off his own, which were casual slip-ons, no socks.

Rather than stare at his naked feet, she trained her gaze on the big surf which was crashing onto a circle of rocks, sending up spectacular sprays, their froth gleaming white in the moonlight. The rocks enclosed a small bay, reducing the waves rolling past them to small swells, a safe swimming area close to the beach.

'Does this place have a name?' she asked, trying to find some normal level with him.

He grinned at her. 'Spoon Bay.'

Laughter gurgled out, easing her nervous tension about accepting whatever would be between them. 'Made for *spooning* by moonlight?'

His eyes twinkled, happy to have her more relaxed with him. 'I think it refers more to the shape of the area…the way the beach curves into the treeline and the rocks curve around the bay. You can't see it properly from here. Come…'

He stood and pulled her to her feet, grabbed the rug again, tucking it under his far arm so he could still hold her hand as they continued down the sand-and-board steps. Catherine took a deep breath of the salty sea air. Somehow it was as intoxicating as the tingling heat of Zack's fingers, intertwining with hers. All her senses seemed switched onto a much sharper level.

They walked along the beach to the little cove Zack had described, sand squishing underfoot, the surf beating out its own primeval rhythm, the almost eerie light of the full moon lending a mood of ancient timelessness to the scene. They could have been the only man and woman in the universe, making footprints where none had been before, surrounded by elements of nature that no human touch had ever controlled.

Would tonight with Zack leaves its imprint on her…a night to remember?

He laid the picnic rug over a stretch of smooth sand in the centre of the cove. The sight of it, ready for them, so *sensible* and *planned,* suddenly put Catherine at odds with its obvious purpose. Her nerves jangled a panicky protest. She tossed her shoes onto it and spun around to face the sea, instinctively seeking a spontaneous rush of something else, more natural, more enticing, more…explosive…like the waves on the rocks, a fierce flow and ebb, driven by mindless forces which were very, very real.

Like what she had felt with Zack before, when he'd kissed her, when…

'Stay right there,' he commanded from behind her, and she heard the rustle and click of his clothes being removed.

She didn't look, couldn't bring herself to look or take any action at all. Her mind filled with a vision of him emerging naked in all his muscular splendour, primal male pulsing with a vitality which he was releasing from all the conventional bonds of their civilised world, and she wanted to be released too, free of all inhibitions. He would come to her…she was waiting…and her heart was drumming louder than the waves now. No turning away from this, no turning…

Her whole body was wire-tight with anticipation when his arms slid around her waist. She almost crumbled at the contact, the need for it was so intense. She leaned back against him, revelling in the sense of being encompassed and protected by his hard, warm strength, wanting to feel a togetherness that could face anything and survive intact. He rubbed his cheek over her hair and she felt his chest rise and fall as he breathed in its scent, mingled now with the smell of the sea.

'You should have been called Eve,' he murmured.

The beginning of time, she thought, elated that he was in tune with her own feelings. 'And you, Adam?'

'The caveman in me has definitely been stirred tonight.'

Was it the cavewoman in her responding? It didn't matter. Having surrendered to whatever it was, she simply wanted to be swept along with it.

His hands slid up to capture her breasts, fingers softly kneading, savouring their fullness. She closed her eyes, inwardly focusing on his touch and the sensations it aroused, the excited tightening of her nipples, the flow of pressures that seemed to make her flesh swell voluptuously and recede in rhythmic waves.

She reached up to pull her hair forward over her shoulders to bare the zipper at the back of her dress, but he didn't do anything about it. He kissed the nape of her neck and glided his hands down over her stomach, her thighs, and gathered up the hem of her dress, lifting the skirt to her waist so the night air shivered over all he'd exposed to it, naked thighs, naked hips, and his palm moved underneath the G-string she still wore, fingers reaching, stroking, building an almost unbearable excitement.

It was unbelievably erotic being caressed like this, without seeing the man who was doing it, only feeling his body behind her, hot flesh pressed to hers while in front of her there was nothing but sand and water and air—elemental nature, swirling, changing, sucking, crashing, wafting—while the fire of desire was being stoked inside her in an echo of the same shifting patterns of movement.

It was wild. And suddenly it was too much for her to keep letting it go on. In a fever of urgency, she dropped her own hands to snatch the flimsy G-string away, pulling it down to step out of it. As she bent over she felt her dress being unzipped, her bra unclipped, and in a few quick seconds, she was completely naked, too, and spun around to face her partner of the night.

He grabbed her hands and stepped back, his eyes feasting on the feminine curves he'd only felt. 'Look at you...'

The awe in his voice filled her own mind as she looked at him, so tall and big and magnificently made in a mould that was utterly perfect manhood.

'...like a siren from the sea, come to lure me away from everything else.'

'Are you a myth?'

'Do I feel like one?'

He lifted her hands to press the palms against his chest, drawing her in to him as he guided them up to his shoulders. The tips of her breasts touched him. Then he released her hands and scooped her into close and intimate contact with all of him.

'Not a myth,' he said gruffly. 'But we can make a legend of tonight, Catherine Trent.'

And he kissed her.... Kissed her as though her mouth held the fountain of life and he thirsted for every drop of it. And she kissed him back with all the pent-up passion from waiting for this, waiting and wanting and needing it to be...just like this.

He swung her off her feet, laid her on the rug, loomed over her, his face ablaze with the fire within, his powerful body dark and taut, rampant male poised to take, primed to take, and a wild elation coursed through Catherine as she positioned herself to possess him.

He came into her with shocking, exhilarating swiftness, the impact of him arching her body in an instinctive and ecstatic urge to hold the deeply penetrating fullness, to have it all, the whole glorious shaft of him imbedded in the warm silky heart of her, surrounding him, enclosing him, drawing him into the ultimate togetherness.

And he paused there to kiss her again, to invade her mouth with the passionate intent to link them in a totality that swam with intense sensation. He was spread on top of her, a pulsing blanket of heated muscle, pressing onto her breasts, their lower bodies locked, her legs wound around his hips, her hands raking his back, her whole body yearning to be utterly joined with his, exulting in feeling everything possible with him.

His arms burrowed under her and she was lifted to straddle his thighs as he sat back on his haunches, his mouth leaving hers to fasten on her breasts, subjecting each one to a wild exquisite suction as he rocked her from side to side, moving the pressure of him inside her to an equally exquisite slide along her inner walls. She threw back her head, instinctively thrusting her breasts forward, loving the hot tug on them, the swirling lash of his tongue on her nipples, and the arc of sweet pleasure that flowed from these ravishing kisses to the tantalising caresses within.

The full moon shone on her face. The sea breeze filtered through her swaying hair. The roar of crashing waves filled her ears. But they were outside things and the vibrant inner life of this union with Zack Freeman swamped her awareness of anything else. It was like an ocean of sensation, whipped by a storm of feeling, tidal waves gathering more and more explosive power.

He surged up and laid her back on the rug, his breath a hot wind on her skin as he hovered over her like a dark mountainous wave about to break. She felt the crest of it, poised within her, holding, holding. Then the pounding began, deep, glorious beats that throbbed through her entire body, convulsing it around him, carrying her into intense turbulence—a turbulence that swept her to an incredible peak of ecstatic excitement, and her body seemed to shatter with the fantastic pleasure of it.

But it wasn't shattered. It floated on rolls of more pleasure, peaking and ebbing, peaking and ebbing, until the driving force of Zack reached its climax on one last brilliant peak and finished in a flood of deep warmth that slowly gentled them both into the sweet peace of utter fulfilment.

They hugged. They kissed. They touched. They revelled in the sensual magic of the night, strolling along the wet sand with the dying froth of waves caressing their feet, swimming in the rock pool, their bodies sliding around each other in the buoyant water, teasing, inviting, savouring the freedom to give and take every pleasure in being together.

To Catherine, he was wonderful. She couldn't have enough of him. And he shared her greed, her lust to have everything possible packed into this one night. Nothing wild was too wild. There was no shame in anything. They loved each other in the water, on the sand, against a rock with the spray of the sea showering over them.

What words were spoken did not relate to any other time or place or circumstance. The past and the future had no bearing on what they shared. There was no breaking of that mutual understanding, no attempt to break it, or change any of the parameters of that one promise…a night to remember.

They didn't sleep.

They left the beach at dawn.

It was time to part.

CHAPTER FIVE

Nine months later…

CATHERINE set the crystal tiara carefully over Livvy's topknot of bright blond curls, watching her sister's reflection in the mirror to position this last piece of wedding finery with perfect precision. 'There!' she said with a satisfied smile, stepping back to fluff out the veil attached to the tiara. 'You look fabulous! A princess bride if ever I saw one.'

Livvy's vivid blue eyes sparkled with happy anticipation. 'I hope Pete thinks so.'

'How could he not?' Catherine's gaze dropped to take in the heavily beaded and embroidered bodice of the wedding dress. It was moulded to every feminine curve like a second skin. Little cap sleeves led into a low heart-shaped neckline, echoed at her tiny waist with a slight dip from which a many-layered tulle skirt frothed to the floor. It was pure romance and typically Livvy. 'You'll take his breath away.'

They shared a sisterhood smile.

'You look fabulous, too, Catherine. That dark red suits you.'

It did. And the simple elegance of the strapless satin sheath was much more her style. Though Livvy had stuck her with a flower in her hair, a dark red rose nestled against the topknot of curls which were more unruly than the bride's but hopefully fastened securely by pins.

All four bridesmaids were wearing their hair up like Livvy's. At the moment, the other three, close friends of her sister, were out of the room, checking out the bouquets which had just been delivered. Livvy seized on the opportunity for a private chat.

'You know what would really make me happy?' she pressed.

'I thought you were over the moon already, marrying the man you love.'

'If you'd just give Kevin a chance. He's Pete's best man. As my chief bridesmaid, you'll be partnered with him and...'

'Please...' Catherine rolled her eyes in exasperation at her sister's persistent matchmaking. '...don't start on that again.'

'But he's really nice. I've met him several times. And he hasn't picked up with anyone since his divorce.'

'You want to land me with a man who has a failed marriage behind him?'

'Now you're being nit-picky. You've got to face it, Catherine. The field of eligible guys narrows down after you're thirty and you've been manless since you finally had the sense to get rid of Stuart Carstairs.'

'And quite contentedly so, thank you. I have my goldfish to keep me company.' She hadn't been allowed to have a dog in her apartment but no one objected to goldfish as pets.

Livvy gritted her teeth. 'Goldfish cannot take the place of a man in your life.'

'You're right. They're something else. Goldfish love you unconditionally. Rhett and Scarlet are always there for me. They're beautiful to look at and they never let me down.'

'Now you're being cynical.'

'Not at all. Just telling it how it is.'

'Rhett and Scarlet,' Livvy scoffed. 'Whoever heard of fish being called after characters from *Gone With the Wind?*'

It seemed apt at the time, since she'd bought them after her night with Zack Freeman…a night that *was* gone with the wind though she'd always remember it.

'At least it shows there's some romance left in your soul,' Livvy reasoned, returning to her pitch. 'Kevin could be good for you.'

Catherine shrugged, not wanting an argument today of all days. 'Well, if he is, he is.'

'So you *will* give him a chance.'

'I'll dance with him at your wedding and hope he doesn't tread on my toes.'

Livvy relaxed into a laugh which ended in a rueful grimace. 'A pity Zack Freeman couldn't make it today. You made such a striking pair when Pete and I fixed up that blind date for the two of you.'

'Mmm…' It was the most non-committal reply Catherine could come up with.

'You know the last big box-office movie that featured his special effects…it's been nominated for a Golden Globe,' Livvy rattled on. 'In my opinion, it's Zack's work that really makes it so dramatic and memorable. Did you go and see it?'

'Yes. Stunning stuff.' She had sat in the movie theatre, enthralled by the mind that could imagine and create such amazing scenes. It had made the night she'd spent with him all the more extraordinary. Uniquely special.

'He might get an Academy Award for that movie,' Livvy rattled on. 'Pete says...'

The other bridesmaids erupted into the room, carrying the bouquets and exclaiming how beautiful they were, and any further talk about Zack Freeman was abruptly dropped, much to Catherine's relief. She didn't want to discuss him or his work. It was easier to keep him tucked away as a private memory.

Initially he'd been designated as Pete's best man, but commitments on the other side of the world had forced him to regretfully decline the honour. Which was undoubtedly true, yet Catherine couldn't help wondering if that suited him since it neatly avoided meeting her again. Though that was probably too personal a slant on his decision. His long friendship with Pete would surely have taken priority over any sense of awkwardness over partnering her again...for just one night.

A second night...

Her stomach clenched at the need that suddenly clawed through her. Stupid, she fiercely told herself. Magic could never be recaptured. It would be different, a second time around. In fact, it might even spoil the memory she had of him. Better that he was caught up in other things elsewhere.

The only problem was, she couldn't get interested in other men, despite her sister's best efforts to couple her with quite a few reasonably attractive prospects. Livvy thought she'd been too scarred by her long relationship with Stuart Carstairs, but it was actually Zack Freeman who got in the way, making other men seem hopelessly pale in comparison.

She hadn't even been tempted to pick up with Stuart again, despite his abject apologies and begging for another chance. In fact, she'd suddenly seen his charm as totally egocentric, a tool he used in a deliberate play for power over others. Manipulation was his game. She'd been blind to it before, or sucked in by feelings he'd known how to play on.

In the first few months after her night with Zack, Stuart had proceeded to target every woman who was professionally associated with Catherine, focusing all his charismatic energy on them, one by one, until he had them, and then he'd slyly let Catherine know as though that was supposed to make her feel jealous or possessive, firing up a desire to have him back in her bed and her life.

It didn't work.

Stuart couldn't get to her anymore.

An ironic little smile hovered on her lips. Zack Freeman had certainly done her a favour there, but had he wrecked any chance of her connecting to someone else who might very well be good for her...like Kevin?

She wandered over to the window, knowing the vintage cars to transport the wedding party were due to arrive. The cars had been Pete's idea, matching up to the old colonial house Livvy had chosen for the reception. All very romantic. As it should be on their wedding day.

The weather had smiled on them. It was a lovely sunny afternoon. The ceremony at the church was scheduled for four o'clock and it was now three-fifteen. Their parents were already dressed and waiting downstairs for their daughters to appear in their wedding finery. They would all leave together from this family home in Lane Cove where Catherine and Livvy had grown up and gone to school.

A big moment for their mother and father, Catherine thought, their younger daughter getting married. Both she and Livvy had left home years ago, seeking more convenient accommodation to their careers and the freedom to lead their lives without too much critical comment from their parents. The independent set-up had freed their parents, too, removing enough of their sense of responsibility and ties to their children for them to really enjoy the travelling they'd always wanted to do. But different lifestyles hadn't diminished the love and caring they shared as a family and today was a milestone to be cherished.

'The cars are coming up the street now,' she announced, glad they wouldn't cause any hitch in the arrangements.

She wanted everything to be perfect for Livvy.

Her sister's wedding.

It might be the only one her family would have. She couldn't see herself ever getting married. For some women there was only ever one man. Catherine suspected hers had been Zack Freeman.

Zack glanced at his watch as he strode out of the Airport Hilton Hotel. Just past three-thirty. He'd flown into Sydney only an hour ago, no luggage to collect since he'd carried his overnight bag and the suit-holder containing his formal clothes for Pete's wedding onto the aircraft with him. He'd shaved in flight so he'd only had to shower and change here at the hotel. With any luck, he should get to the church on time.

The taxi he'd ordered was waiting for him. He climbed into it and gave the driver the address at Chatswood, adding that he had to be there by four o'clock for a wedding.

'No worries,' the cabbie cheerfully assured him. 'We take the freeway and the harbour tunnel. Being Saturday afternoon, the traffic's not heavy. In any event, the bride is always late.'

Not Livvy, Zack thought, remembering her on-the-dot punctuality in arriving at the Galley restaurant on the night of his blind date with Catherine.

Catherine...

He sighed over the frustrating conflicts she raised in his mind. The memory of her had almost stopped him from coming to this wedding. *Pete's* wedding! As it was, he'd let his old friend down, declining the role of best man because that would have inevitably put him as Catherine's partner in the wedding party.

He shook his head over her lingering and pervasive effect on him. Try as he might, he couldn't set the memory of that one night with her aside and it had proved unsettling too many times over this past year, distracting him from business, insidiously destroying the attraction that other women would have had in the normal course of events. But he should not have let it get in the way of standing up for Pete on his wedding day.

His hands clenched in anger.

Bad decision!

When he'd called from Singapore last night to say he *was* coming, the excitement and pleasure in Pete's voice had shamed him...letting a woman—any woman—put him off sharing in such an important day. Their friendship was worth more than any disturbance Catherine Trent might give him.

'I may be late getting there,' he'd warned.

'Hey! No problem, man. It'll be great to see you. I'll tell Mum to organise a seat for you at the reception. Where would you like to be? With the young bloods?'

He should have been sitting beside Pete. Since he'd given up that place and weddings were really a family affair, he'd answered, 'No. With my mother, if that's possible. Haven't seen her for a while.'

'Done.'

And that had made him feel guilty, too. Pete would oblige him with anything, and he'd...too late to rue it now. Damn Livvy's sister and her power to mess with things that were not related to her. He hoped seeing her again today would put the memory of that one night with her in some reasonable perspective. Get it out of his system.

His mother was always good company. She would claim his attention. Now there was one woman he did genuinely love. She'd always stuck up for him against his father who'd relentlessly put him down, jeering over his interest in computer graphics, saying he was wasting his time and would never amount to anything. Too bad he'd died when Zack was only twenty. Though he'd probably even deride what his son had achieved if he was still alive.

Zack didn't grieve over the loss of his father, though he would have liked the chance to shove his success down the old man's throat. Domineering narrow-minded bastard! Why his mother had stayed in that marriage all those years was beyond his understanding. He'd watched his father crush the joy out of her countless times, though she'd stubbornly clung to what she believed in, opposing him when it was important to her.

Thirteen years she'd been widowed now, and showed no inclination to look for another husband. It was probably a relief to be absolutely free to do as she liked and not have to justify or account to anyone for what she did. She filled her life with things she enjoyed; running the arts and crafts gallery at Dora Creek, playing bridge with Pete's mum twice a week, still doing her own pottery. She was a lovely person with a large circle of friends and she'd always insisted to Zack that she wasn't lonely.

'Follow your star wherever it takes you,' she'd told him many times. 'Fulfilling what you most want to do is what gives your life meaning. Go for it, Zack. Don't let anyone stop you.'

He hadn't.

But his focus on what he was going for had been knocked slightly awry by Catherine Trent and he intended to correct that today. It was absurd that one night with her still had the capacity to tie him in knots. He had to get this...*aberration*...straightened out. No way was he ready to get tied up with any woman.

The taxi was emerging from the harbour tunnel. Zack checked his watch again. Ten minutes left to get there. He'd probably arrive at the same time as the bride. Which would mean seeing Catherine as Livvy's bridesmaid. He felt his nerves tightening and willed them to relax.

She wouldn't stun him a second time.

He knew what she looked like.

A nod of acknowledgment or a wave as he headed

into the church would get him by. More than likely, he'd find she didn't match up to the memory and this whole *thing* about her would fade into insignificance. They'd shared a great night, but that was all it was...one great night.

He dismissed it from his mind, determined to concentrate on Pete and Livvy. He hoped they'd have a good marriage and the children they both wanted. Maybe that had been part of the problem with his parents, his mother only able to have one child and Zack hadn't been the kind of son his father had wanted...no interest in going into boat-building or taking up a *useful* trade. If there'd been other sons...

Though Pete had been an only son, too, and his father had been happy to let him go his own way. Maybe having two daughters, as well, had softened him. Zack had always liked going to the Raynor home. No-one there had ever criticised his and Pete's absorption in computer games. Pete had loved the challenge of *winning*. Zack had been fascinated by the graphics, wanting to know how they were done and how they could be done better.

They were good times.

'Church coming up,' the cabbie informed him. 'And from the look of the three highly polished vintage cars ahead of us, the bridal party is just arriving.'

Zack smiled at the choice of cars—bound to be Pete's idea. His first car had been an old rattletrap MG which he'd insisted was a classic. Zack had bought his first motorbike—secondhand—at about the same time. Lots of shared memories with Pete, and today would be another one, as it should be.

The vintage cars pulled into a driveway by the side

of the church and came to a processional halt. The chauffeurs were hopping out to open the back doors for their passengers as the taxi passed by and pulled in at the street kerb adjacent to the gate which was the public entrance to the churchyard. Zack quickly paid over the fare, adding a generous tip to thank the cabbie for the timely arrival.

He was out of the taxi and at the gate when a man emerged from the lead car, his age and the flower in the lapel of his black suitcoat marking him as Livvy's father. Movement at the opened door of the second car caught his eye. He deliberately kept heading for the vestibule of the church, trying to crush the urge to look. This was Pete's day. Catherine Trent was a side issue.

'Wait for me to help, Dad.'

The seductive lilt of her voice tempted him.

'Now, Catherine, I'm the father of the bride. Don't do me out of my job.'

She laughed.

That did it.

He stopped and looked.

She'd taken a couple of steps towards the lead car and was swinging towards him, looking at the ground to be covered from the bride's car to the church. Her head jerked in shock at her first sight of him. Disbelief chased across her face.

Now was the time to nod or wave and move right on by, Zack told himself. But his body didn't obey that dictate. She stared at him and he stared at her, both of them totally immobile. It was as if they were caught in a time-warp where only they existed, bonded together by memories that were uniquely theirs.

She was vividly, vibrantly, and undeniably stunning…so beautiful he couldn't tear his gaze away. Her hair was piled on top of her head and he remembered her holding it there like that after they'd been swimming, inadvertantly showing off the long graceful curve of her neck which he'd kissed many times.

She had a flower in her hair again, dark red this time, not pink. The same dark red as the dress she was wearing, a strapless dress that bared her shoulders and arms, the hollow at the base of her neck, and the slight swell of flesh that hinted at the lush fullness of her breasts.

His mouth went dry, remembering the tight texture of her nipples, the salty taste of them in the sea. His hands itched to span her provocatively small waist, to run them over the voluptuous curve of her hips, down the long silky line of her thighs. He could feel himself stirring, the desire she evoked zinging through his bloodstream, pumping up an urgent need to have her again.

'Zack!' The call of his name snapped the dangerous thrall. It came from Livvy, stepping out of her car in a cloud of white. 'You came!' she cried in surprised delight. 'Does Pete know?'

He nodded. He waved a salute to her. It felt as though he was reacting in slow motion. Words finally came. 'See you in the church.'

He didn't risk another look at Catherine. His legs took him where he had to go. A church was supposed to be a safe haven. It felt like a trap but there was no escape from it. He was here for Pete.

Catherine gave herself a mental shake. Zack Freeman *was* here. It hadn't been a hallucination. Livvy had seen him, too. Spoken to him. And he'd answered. He'd come for the wedding, was in the church right now, waiting for it to begin.

The way he'd looked at her…her whole body was still tingling. Despite the most part of a year having passed since their one night together, it had felt as though time had stood still and the intimate connection was just as immediate and powerful as it had been then. No difference at all. And her heart was skittering all over the place at the thought of having another night with him.

But he wasn't her partner tonight.

She had to be with…what was his name? Kevin.

Not *all* the time, she thought fiercely.

Her mind trembled at the enormity of what she was thinking and feeling. He hadn't made any contact with her. He'd come to the wedding out of friendship with Pete. Yet given the chance, she *would* choose to be with Zack Freeman.

All night.

CHAPTER SIX

CATHERINE ached from the tension of waiting for Zack to make some move on her. She couldn't bring herself to accept that he wasn't going to, yet how else could she explain the distance he had kept from her. He was with his mother, she kept telling herself, but surely no mother expected her adult son to give her his exclusive attention.

Besides, it hadn't been entirely exclusive. After the wedding ceremony, there'd been a photo session outside the church. Zack had emerged from the milling guests, headed straight for the just married couple, shook Pete's hand, kissed the bride, a dazzling smile accompanying his congratulations, but the smile hadn't been turned on Catherine. He hadn't even looked at her.

With her heart turning over with disappointment, she'd watched him go to Pete's parents and chat to them, then move to the side of a very stylish middle-aged woman whom she now knew to be his mother, though she didn't look at all like Zack with her fly-away auburn hair, fair skin and green eyes.

Nevertheless, Pete had identified her as such, and Catherine had decided it was fair enough for Zack to put his mother first, particularly since her own role as chief bridesmaid had kept her busy; seeing that Livvy was posed perfectly for the photographs, then helping her into the car with Pete, ensuring the billowing layers of tulle didn't get caught on anything. Zack, she had then argued to herself, was probably waiting until she had some time to herself.

There'd been another much longer session with the photographer in the lovely garden setting at Wisteria House where the reception had been booked. The two-storeyed Colonial home had wonderful verandas, their supporting columns skirted by ornate white lace ironwork. Guests had been invited onto the upper veranda to watch all the formal posing in the garden while they were served cocktails and hors d'oeuvres.

Several times Catherine had felt Zack's gaze burning into her, but when she'd glanced up at the onlooking crowd, his attention was not focused on her at all.

Pete had called him down, insisting he wanted a shot of Zack with himself and Livvy. He'd obliged his old friend but laughingly declined posing for a foursome with Catherine. 'Not my place,' he'd excused. 'Get the best man for that shot.' And he was gone again, leaving Catherine with the feeling he was avoiding any contact with her.

Yet why would that be so?

She hadn't chased him, hadn't made a nuisance of herself. At the end of the night they'd shared, she hadn't tried to cling on or press for some further involvement with him. Did he fear she would now? Make some kind of scene he'd hate? Or…her stomach cramped at the thought…had he met some other woman he wanted to keep? It would explain why he'd refused to be linked to Catherine in a photograph.

The torment of not knowing what he was thinking plagued her all through the reception dinner. Despite his stopping by the bridal table a couple of times to chat to Pete, Zack didn't once switch his attention to her. The only evidence that he hadn't completely forgotten their blind date and its intimate aftermath was the one long sizzling look outside the church, and that certainly wasn't being repeated.

Catherine doggedly ate what was put in front of her, assured Livvy the food was great without knowing whether it was or not, forced adequate responses to the general chat at the bridal table, smiled when a smile was expected.

She sat through the speeches without hearing a word, though her gaze remained fixed on each speaker as though she was listening avidly. But she was dying inside, drowning in a sea of painful confusion and frustration. She could only hope no one noticed. It was her sister's wedding.

Zack gritted his teeth, fighting the surge of violence that urged him to wipe the smirk off the best man's face, tear his arm from Catherine's waist, and break the fingers that were feeling their way up the erotic curve of her spine.

'She's very beautiful.'

His mother's voice filtered through the battle roar in his ears. He wrenched his gaze from the couple on the dance floor and managed a foggy look.

'What?' he asked, not having caught what she was talking about.

An amused smile teased his loss of rapport with her. 'Livvy's sister, Catherine. Don't tell me you haven't noticed how striking she is. You've been fixated on her all evening.'

He frowned, not liking to think his *obsession* with Catherine Trent was obvious. 'She is…very watchable,' he said, trying to brush the issue aside.

'You don't have to stay with me, Zack. I am with friends and they'll look after me. Feel free to pursue your interest in her.'

'I don't have the time for it,' he stated dismissively.

Her eyes gently mocked his assertion. 'Haven't you climbed your mountain? Doesn't it get lonely at the top by yourself?'

He mocked right back. 'Just because Pete's got himself married today doesn't mean I'm ready for it.'

'You make it sound as if it has to be programmed into your schedule.'

'For the best outcome…yes, it does. Nothing works well unless you've planned for it.'

She laughed. 'Do you really think you can plan love, Zack? That you can snap your fingers and…hey presto! The woman you want as your partner for life will roll up and present herself just when you want her to?'

He shrugged. 'I'll put my mind to it when I feel the need.' It certainly wasn't love on his mind right now. More a case of lust raging out of control.

Still looking highly amused, his mother said, 'You can't will it, either. It happens. You can't order the time, the place or the person. It simply…happens.'

'You're talking chemistry, not love,' he answered dryly.

'Am I? Well, let me pose you a question, Zack. Food for thought. How many Catherine Trents have you met?'

Only one. And one was too many, messing with his life.

His mother didn't wait for a reply.

It was his business, his decision.

She pushed back her chair and stood up, off-handedly stating, 'I think I'll find the powder room.'

His gaze instantly targeted the dance floor. Other couples were jigging apart, happily putting their own steps to the beat of the music. Not Catherine and her partner, who was all too conveniently no taller than she was. The guy had her thighs glued to his, and the hand now spread over the lower slope of the pit of her back was definitely applying pressure.

A red haze of fury tinged Zack's thoughts. He knew dancing wasn't on Kevin Macy's mind. More like wet dreams. The guy undoubtedly had an erection. Any minute now he'd be dancing Catherine out the opened French doors, finding a shadowed place on the veranda…

His chair almost tipped over as Zack erupted onto his feet. It had taken iron control not to make any connection with Catherine Trent this time around, but be damned if he was going to let some other guy connect with her right under his nose. He barely

stopped himself from charging like a bull, head
down, nostrils steaming, horns lowered ready to gore.
It was certainly how he felt.

Catherine knew she should stop what Kevin Macy
was doing. She'd slid into a careless passive state,
too drained of energy to bother forcing a break away
from him. Nevertheless, being nice to him did not
include allowing him this *frottage* on the dance floor.
It was getting downright dirty and he was probably
nursing ideas she didn't want to encourage.

He was not the man for her.

He never would be.

And she didn't care if Livvy scolded her for not
grabbing what was available. All too available,
Catherine thought grimly, screwing up the strength
to make a few things clear to Kevin Macy. Just as
she was lifting her gaze to his face, she saw a hand
clamp over his shoulder, a strong darkly toned hand,
its fingers bent like lethal claws, digging into Kevin's
suitcoat.

Her heart instantly skipped a beat.

'Hey!' Kevin protested, loosening his grip on her
as he half turned to face the threatened assault.

Zack Freeman glowered at him from his intimi-
dating height, the power of his physique a ready de-
terrent to any argument, though he didn't need it. The
aggressive energy he emitted was enough to drop
Kevin's jaw and kill any further words Pete's best
man might have spoken.

'Excuse me,' Zack grated out, his dark eyes blazing a challenge that would have shrivelled any last

scrap of foolhardy courage. 'This dance with Catherine is mine.'

Kevin not only didn't dispute the claim, he didn't even check with Catherine if she wanted to be passed over to Zack. He dropped her like a hot coal and back-tracked off the dance floor, gesturing for Zack to take her over. Which he did, with a speed that almost swept her off her feet. Pressed to another male body—a very different male body—Catherine struggled against the flood of excitement it stirred, a rebellious sense of pride insisting that she shouldn't surrender to it willy-nilly.

'You didn't ask my permission,' she fired at him, her eyes defying his arrogance in assuming he could keep her waiting for hours and still do whatever he wanted with her.

'No, I didn't.' He returned her challenge with blistering mockery. 'You can reject me if you want to.'

She burned. From head to toe she burned with the need to be with him. To deny it would be completely self-defeating. 'I hear you've had a good year,' she said, moving to less contentious ground and being deliberately bland so he wouldn't know her whole body was aquiver from being in contact with his again.

'A very good year,' he answered, his chin tilting belligerently, his eyes blazing with self-determination.

'That must give you a lot of satisfaction,' she ran on, suddenly hating the fact that she'd had no part in it, hadn't been invited to take any part in it.

'Yes,' he acknowledged, but the mockery was

back, deriding this conversation, telling her it had no relevance.

It goaded her into demanding some recognition of her as a person, not just the object of a desire he could pick up and put down as he liked. 'Why don't you ask me about my year?'

'Because I don't want to know.'

Ruthless truth.

He only wanted to *know* her in the biblical sense. She averted her gaze from the intensely raw penetration of his and writhed through the shame of blushing like a schoolgirl.

'It's trivia, Catherine, and it won't change anything,' he stated harshly.

'Well, my life might be trivia to you but it's not trivia to me,' she flashed back at him, a fierce resentment surging at his dismissive attitude.

His eyes narrowed, weighing the strength of her attack and whether it was worth his while to make any concession to it. 'So what do you want to tell me?' he demanded. 'Give me the important highlights.'

There were none. Her job had provided a few little triumphs—winning accounts against strong competition—but they were hardly huge highlights that would make her shine for him. Her personal life was virtually a void, although she had taken up yoga and done a course in Italian cooking, both activities giving her considerable satisfaction. She wasn't about to admit that her experience with him had put her off other men.

'I bought two goldfish,' she tossed out, not caring

about his definition of trivia. Rhett and Scarlet had become the one daily constant in her private life since he had left it and she loved having them to come home to.

He looked startled, then bemused. 'Two goldfish,' he repeated with mock gravity.

'Yes.' She tilted her chin to a challenging angle. 'And I bought a beautiful bowl for them to swim in.'

His mouth burst into a wide, dazzling grin. Then he threw back his head and laughed, startling her with his wild amusement. He clasped her closer, whirling her around, his thighs driving them both across the dance floor in a flurry of steps that carved a path through the crowd of other dancers, out past the opened French doors and onto the veranda.

The cooler night air did nothing to lessen the heat Zack Freeman generated in her. 'That wasn't meant to be funny,' she protested, feeling intensely vulnerable now that they weren't completely surrounded by people. He had danced her down to the far end of the veranda, away from the other guests who were grouped around the door or leaning against the wrought-iron balustrade nearby.

His dark eyes twinkled amusement as he answered, 'Only you would tell me about goldfish, Catherine.' His chest heaved against her breasts and his slowly expelled breath tingled over her upturned face. 'Only you...' he repeated, his deep voice lowered to a caressing murmur.

Thinking of all the high-flying women he surely met while doing international business in the movie world, Catherine muttered, 'I don't lead your kind of exciting life.'

He shook his head as though she hadn't grasped his meaning. He seemed about to say more, stopped, grimaced, then flatly answered, 'The pace is tough. I'm on a flight back to London in the morning, Catherine. I only came for Pete's wedding.'

Fair warning…like last time…and if she had any sense she would walk away from him right now because it meant—as before—he had no intention of involving himself in an ongoing relationship with her. It was here now, gone tomorrow, no different to their first night together. Yet even knowing this, Catherine could not quash the feelings he aroused.

'It was good of you to make the time. Pete is so pleased you came,' she said in an equally flat tone, her lashes sweeping down to hide the emotional conflict of wanting far more than he was ever likely to give her, yet not wanting to turn away from him.

She stared at his bow tie sitting neatly at the base of his neck and wished she was a vampire, able to sink her teeth into his jugular vein and get into his bloodstream so powerfully he could never shake free of her. Her heart was thumping with the need to hold him to her any way she could. Her hands curled, the urge to claw and dig in sweeping through her in a fierce wave, driving her nails into her palms to stop such primitive and futile action.

'I'm sure your mother is, too,' she forced herself to add, a biting reminder of the hours of torment she had already suffered on his account. Zack Freeman was not going to be swayed from his course. There was no chance of anything more than another brief encounter with him.

He hadn't introduced her to his mother.

Didn't that tell her she was nothing but a bit of fluff on the side to him?

So stop this now.

Stop it and do the walking away herself.

Before she gave her heart and soul to him again.

Though weren't they his already?

'My mother thinks you're very beautiful,' he murmured.

It jolted her into looking up, meeting the simmering warmth in his eyes. 'You talked about me...to her?'

'She's right. You are.' His mouth curved into a sensual little smile. 'Irresistibly so.'

His head dipped towards hers. A kiss was coming. Her heart catapulted around her chest. Her mind screamed that this was the moment to stop him. But her whole body yearned to feel again how it was with him and when his mouth touched hers there was no thought left of pulling back. Any last shred of denial was swamped by a rush of blood to the head, blood that sang for all the sensations she craved.

Yes...it was a lilt of exultation as the desire for passionate possession exploded between them.

Yes...it was a fierce throb of satisfaction as his arms crushed her into an intimate awareness of the power of his need.

Yes...it was a paean of triumph that all the barriers that had separated them were being comprehensively smashed.

They kissed and were united in a deep inner world of their own, feverishly claiming all they could while they could—a savage feast of kissing, of touching, of immersing all their senses in each other. But it was never going to be enough out here on a public veranda in open view of anyone who chanced to look their way. That frustration did eventually break into the headlong rush to recapture all they had spent so many months remembering…or trying to forget.

'I have a room booked at the Airport Hilton Hotel,' Zack breathed in her ear. 'Come with me after the wedding is over.'

A hotel room…

Catherine's emotional recoil was instant.

No!

It would make her feel like a callgirl, visiting a totally impersonal room for sex, and an airport hotel hammered home how fleeting that visit would be. Yet she could not bear not to have him for as long as she could.

'My apartment,' she swiftly countered, pulling back from him to plead her choice. 'It's at Randwick. Not far from Mascot Airport. We could go there. Then I won't feel so bad when you have to leave in the morning.'

He frowned. 'I don't want to make you feel bad, Catherine.'

'I'd hate waking up alone in a hotel room, Zack,' she rushed out, panicking at the thought he might withdraw from any further intimacy. Sharing pleasure was his agenda, not giving pain. 'I'd rather wake up to my goldfish,' she quickly added, hoping that would amuse him again.

The frown cleared as his mouth quirked into a smile. 'I could get jealous of those fish.'

'I don't kiss them.'

'I'm relieved to hear it.'

He kissed her again, a slow sensual promise of what was to come in the hours they would have together. In her home, Catherine thought with dizzy joy. Which would make it all the more real, more intimate, more memorable. Taking him there, having him there, grounded him in surroundings that were hers and hers alone.

'I'll order a car to be waiting for us,' Zack murmured, his voice furred with the desire he had to contain for a little while longer. 'As soon as Pete and Livvy take their leave...'

'Yes,' she agreed, and despite knowing he would be gone in the morning, she could not quell the hope in her heart.

Zack Freeman still wanted her.

He might always want her.

CHAPTER SEVEN

ZACK didn't like the idea of going to Catherine's apartment. He cursed himself for not having thought anything through before taking her from Kevin Macy. Now, finally, they were at the farewell stage of the wedding with Pete and Livvy circling the guests before going off on their honeymoon. The car he'd ordered was waiting at the gates to Wisteria House, and Zack was faced with taking Catherine home, to a place she would have made distinctly her own, and that was getting too close to her.

He was awake to what it meant when a woman invited him to her home ground. It gave her the sense of having some kind of propriety rights over him. As a general rule he avoided the situation, offering a less personal get-together or making some excuse to be elsewhere. The problem was, he'd never wanted a woman as much as he wanted Catherine Trent. He'd given in to her wish with barely a hesitation, driven by the compulsion to have her under any circumstances, not even caring about consequences.

It was stupid.

He'd end up paying dearly for it, too. She'd be etched more deeply in his mind, the memory of her nagging at him when he didn't want to be nagged. Yet even knowing all this, he couldn't bring himself to stop what had been arranged between them. She was standing by her mother, right at the doorway which led to the staircase and out of here. Just a few more minutes…

'Zack, old buddy…' Pete clapped his shoulder and shook his hand vigorously. 'Thanks for coming. Really appreciate it.'

Pete looked drunk with happiness. Getting married to Livvy was certainly sitting well with him. 'You're hooked, man, but I guess the bait was worth taking,' Zack said, grinning at his old friend.

'Right on!' Pete agreed smugly. 'Beat you to it, Zack.'

A typically competitive remark, but there was no race being run here. Not in Zack's mind. Marriage was way down the track for him, though when he looked back at Catherine, his mother's words did beg the question—how often was a guy struck as hard as this by a woman?

He was aching to hold her again.

But that would pass once he'd had his fill of her. Just strong chemistry, he told himself. In fact, going to her apartment might be a good thing, reducing their connection to something ordinary. Not like his memories of their intimacy at the beach. That had been such a fantastic experience it wouldn't be human not to remember it as something special. Tonight would be different. Not that he wanted her any less, but her bedroom was not an evocative setting of sand and sea and moonlight.

'I guess you'll be off as soon as Pete goes,' his mother said.

'Yes.' He tore his gaze from Catherine to pay his

respect to the woman who'd always stood by him through thick and thin. She was literally standing by him now and he gave her a hug and a kiss on the cheek. 'It was good to see you, Mum.'

'Don't stay on your mountain too long, Zack,' she said wistfully. 'There's more of life to live. I'm going to envy Pete's mother her grandchildren.'

He frowned at the sentiment she had never voiced before. It was the wedding, focusing her thoughts on family, he reasoned. Though he was her only child. Had that been a sorrow to her? Did she long for more children through him? Yet she'd always preached he had his own life to live and set him free to do it, as free as any mother could.

He shook his head as his gaze swung back to Catherine. He wasn't ready for marriage and he wasn't ready to father children. Both were serious commitments. He'd give them his best shot when the time came but that wasn't now. There were industry awards coming up that he could capitalise on big-time. And he would.

This night with Catherine was a brief time-out. He wasn't about to let it become anything more. She knew the score, didn't she? He didn't want to leave her feeling bad.

She was kissing Livvy goodbye. The bride moved on to her parents—the last farewell. Catherine looked at him, her sexy golden-amber eyes gleaming with the same sizzling impatience he felt.

Mutual desire.

No question she wanted what he wanted.

He wasn't doing any wrong by her.

There could be no harm in just one more night.

And the pleasure... Zack sucked in a quick breath...hours of it...with Catherine Trent.

It wasn't a taxi waiting for them. It was a chauffeured Mercedes with plush leather seats. Very comfortable, but Catherine couldn't relax. Since the law demanded they wear seat belts Zack wasn't about to pounce, yet she half wished he would because she was so painfully tense and she needed her doubts and fears obliterated.

Arrow signs to the airport kept flashing at Catherine on their way to Randwick, relentlessly reminding her that Zack would be heading there in just a few more hours...and possibly reminding him of the convenience of his hotel room, raising questions about the wisdom of going with her to her apartment, getting further involved with a woman he'd deliberately shunned for most of the wedding.

What if the impulse to pursue the desire they shared waned before they reached her place? How strong was it on his side? If he stayed with her for the rest of the night...if it was as incredibly wonderful as last time...would he come back for more of what they felt together...again and again and again? Or was that a hopeless pipedream on her part?

He was holding her hand, his thumb moving restlessly over her knuckles, back and forth, back and forth. A fine tension held them both silent. A huge wave of relief washed through Catherine when the car finally diverted from the route to the airport and headed past Centennial Park to where she'd been liv-

ing since landing her current job five years ago.
Almost home now. Her fear that Zack might change
his mind about spending the night with her began to
ease.

The urge to babble something that might be of
interest to him raised feverish streams of thought.
The company she worked for, Wavelength
Promotions, had its offices at Botany, only a ten-
minute drive from her apartment. She could be telling Zack this, relating her own experience with computer graphic designs, the presentations she made to
clients. It was the normal thing to do. Yet his hard
words—*I don't want to know*—held her tongue-tied.
Perhaps he was right and only the feeling between
them was important. Just…let it be.

The car arrived at her address. Zack spoke to the
chauffeur, making arrangements for a car to pick him
up here at 6:00 a.m., giving his mobile phone number
for a cross-check with the hire company. Catherine
wasn't quick enough to memorise the numbers. Not
that it would do any good, she told herself. It was
up to Zack to make any future contact. Meanwhile,
she now knew precisely how long he would stay with
her this time. Six o'clock…sunrise…

She desperately wanted to make a lasting impres-
sion on him, something more meaningful than whatever affairs he'd had with other women. Though her
mind was helplessly foggy on how to accomplish
that, especially when communication between them
was overwhelmingly physical. Even as Zack followed her up the central staircase of the apartment
block to her door on the first floor, his footsteps be-

hind her made her heart beat faster and her legs feel tremulous.

Lucky that she hid a spare door key in the artificial aspidistra that dressed up a corner of the lobby serving the two apartments on her floor. She'd left her handbag at her parents' home at Lane Cove. Having untaped the key from the back of one of the plastic leaves, she quickly shoved it into the door lock and opened the way for Zack to enter her private space.

'Not the safest place in the world to keep a key,' he dryly commented.

'Green tape,' she explained. 'Unless you know where to look it's not easily found.'

'You let me know.'

'You're flying out, Zack,' she reminded him. 'I don't see you as a danger to me or mine.'

He frowned at her as he stepped past into the small living room. 'Don't be too free with your trust, Catherine. You're at risk...a woman like you living alone in the city.'

Having extracted the key from the lock, she closed the door and pointedly slotted home the safety chain. 'A woman like me takes care of herself,' she lilted, turning to him with a smile. 'But thank you for your concern, Zack.'

It wasn't just sex. He cared about her feelings, cared about her safety. The secret hope she nursed— that he might come to love her—danced a lively quickstep.

Zack thought her self-assurance vastly misplaced. Didn't she realise how sexy and desirable she was?

Any red-blooded man would feel attracted, excited, simply by the sight of her. She had everything that incited lust, a body that curved so provocatively a guy would have to be dead not to want to touch it, a face that fascinated with its feminine mystique, and hair...

That red rose had been teasing him all night. He wanted to pluck it out, rake his fingers through the cluster of curls, scattering the pins that confined them, and wind whole skeins of her long silky hair around his hands, revelling in the feel of it and binding her to him in an inescapable hold.

She pushed away from the door in a skittish rush. 'Let me introduce you to my fish.'

Fish! What she needed was a big brute of a dog—a Doberman pinscher or a German shepherd—trained to go for the jugular of anyone who threatened her peace of mind.

'Why fish?' he demanded. 'Why not a dog? Pete told me your sister's got a dog.'

She'd hurried straight past him. The question made her pause, glance back, and he was struck again by the seductive line of her neck and shoulder...soft, bare, vulnerable, asking to be kissed.

'We're not allowed dogs in this building.'

The body corporate wielding rules and regulations. Zack grimaced at the imposed constraints. Not many freedoms left in city living. But at least they now had the freedom of complete privacy. He moved to close in on Catherine, determined on soothing the nervous agitation which had suddenly seized her once the door to the outside world had been shut.

Her head snapped forward and she gestured to the fishbowl in front of her. 'The gold one is Rhett, and the red-gold one is Scarlet,' she said in a breathless flurry.

He spanned her waist with his hands—intensely satisfying—and smiled at her choice of names. 'Are they destined to have an unhappy end as in *Gone With the Wind?*'

'No. They…'

He licked her earlobe, nibbled on it. She wore an enticing musky perfume that sharply stirred his senses. He tasted her skin…

Catherine scooped in a quick breath. '…they chase each other endlessly around the bowl. I think Rhett and Scarlet did that, even after the book ended.'

'Perhaps they simply feel trapped.' He released her waist and slowly ran his fingertips up her arms, a feather-light touch that gave her the freedom to move if she wanted to. She didn't. She held herself completely still and the tiny little tremors under her skin told him how sensitive she was to his touch.

Another swift intake of breath. 'No. They're happy fish,' she insisted.

'How do you know?'

He trailed his fingers up her neck, over the soft thickness of her pinned-up hair to the dark red rose.

'Because I watch them play. They like their bowl. Its hexagonal shape is good Feng Shui, promoting peace and harmony. They have fun pushing the pebbles around at the bottom and the aquarium plants offer ready food beyond what I feed them. They're *happy* fish.'

He'd tucked the rose in his breast pocket and was pulling out the hairpins. 'Well, I guess they have eight views of the world from their hexagonal bowl, and many of them would be of you, so I'd call them fortunate fish.'

No reply this time. Absolute stillness.

'And very exotic. Like their owner,' he added, feeling her breath-held tension as he loosened the upswept curls and gently massaged her scalp. Her taut submissiveness tempered the fire of need burning through him with a strange flood of tenderness. Instead of hurling the hairpins away and stripping her naked as fast as he could, he tucked them into his pocket behind the rose, then simply enjoyed the spill of her hair, cascading over his hands and arms, brushing her shoulders, tumbling down her back… beautiful, glossy, excitingly sensual…

'You think I'm…exotic?' The husky lilt suggested that Catherine's mind had only just caught on to that word and didn't know how to process it.

'Uh-huh…a rare, exquisite creature with glorious hair and golden eyes.' He stepped around to face her, smiling over the truths he'd just spoken. He lifted her hair up on either side of her face, then let it slide through his fingers to float around her like a living fan. 'Perhaps you don't know how rare you are, Catherine, but I do. I do,' he repeated as desire surged again at the soft, hazy wonderment in her eyes…such a sensuous look, fringed by the long thick lashes that brushed his face when they kissed.

Her lips were slightly parted, lushly inviting, irresistible. He gathered her in…this woman who struck chords that made him almost a stranger to himself...and kissed her with a sense of exploring new territory, wanting to know what it meant, how it was, where it was taking him, and why it was so different to all he had known before.

No need for any haste. He had hours to take her all in, sift through the feelings she aroused, define them, understand them. With understanding came control and Zack *wanted* control over the effect Catherine Trent had on him.

Yet even as he kissed her with a conscious seeking in his mind, he could feel his quest for control melting under the sweet taunting heat of her lips and tongue. The addictive possession of her mouth burned his brain cells. His whole body burned to be inside her, enveloped by the velvet heat he knew was waiting for him. Only the most ingrained discipline drove him to check what had to be checked. It took an act of will to withdraw from the intoxicating fusion of desire long enough to breathe out the necessary words.

'Is it safe, Catherine?'

She didn't reply. Her face remained tilted to his, her lips parted enough for a soft waft of breath to escape, her eyes closed as though all her senses were focused inward, poised to respond to whatever he did. She wasn't listening to anything but the fire raging within, the fire that could so quickly flare into a furnace, consuming them both to the exclusion of everything else.

'Catherine...' he groaned, his whole body screaming against any pause for precaution. 'I didn't bring any condoms with me. I didn't plan...' He was admitting her power to draw him beyond any limits he imposed, but right at this moment he didn't care. 'Is it safe?' he asked raggedly, begging for a *yes*, because any negative now would be intolerable. Impossible to shut down on the blinding urge to take her, have her.

Safe?

Her stomach curled a fierce protest at Zack's caution as her mind reluctantly came to grips with the question. Condoms...contraception...she'd been off the pill for months. No need for it. And Zack hadn't been expected at the wedding. She hadn't anticipated being tempted.

But if she said no....

Panic and rebellion rolled through her. She couldn't let him leave her, not when she was only assured of one night with him. It couldn't stop now. The yearning for some fulfilment of her need screamed at her to lie.

Though it might not be a lie. Where was she in her monthly cycle? She couldn't think. It didn't matter. She could take the morning-after pill tomorrow if there was a risk of pregnancy. She didn't have to lie.

'Yes,' she said on a heady gasp of release from caring about any unwanted consequences. 'Safe.'

Yet it was a lie.

Catherine knew in her heart there was nothing safe about what she was doing with Zack Freeman tonight. She would give him all she had to offer because he drew that from her as no man ever had before, but he might very well take her body, break her heart, and leave her soul empty.

Tomorrow he would be gone again.

Tomorrow she would think about what to risk and what not to risk.

CHAPTER EIGHT

RELIEF curbed the aggression that had gripped Zack, virtually compelling an abandonment of all caution. *Safe* meant there was nothing to fight. *Safe* meant uninhibited pleasure. Safe meant there would be no shadows on his freedom, once this night was over.

He forced himself to relax, determined on regaining control. He didn't want to be swept headlong into the final act of sex within the first few minutes of having Catherine to himself. Much better to savour the excitement of anticipation, take the time to explore every facet of his fascination with her, know all of her so totally there would be no curiosity left to taunt or haunt him in the future.

Softly, slowly, he kissed her closed eyes, feeling the slight flutter of her long lashes brush his chin, a butterfly touch he fancied on other parts of his body. Was she still nervous about her decision to have him? Her tension in the car had been palpable, and using the fish as an almost frantic distraction from his presence here in her apartment were both signs of uncertainty...or apprehension.

She could have said no, Zack argued to himself, and her response to his kiss just now was enough assurance that the desire they shared overrode any doubts or fears, but it suddenly niggled that she might not be fully with him. He could take her. She was willing. But he didn't want any part of her to be withheld from him.

He lifted his hands and gently cupped her face, studying its unique feminine contours, her marble-smooth forehead, the fine arch of her brows with their winged ends, the deeply set lids that gave her eyes their exotic triangular shape, the high slanted cheekbones flanking her neat straight nose, the seductive fullness of her perfectly shaped lips...

She opened her eyes, the dark pupils so large their amber rims looked like rings of gold. Zack felt his heart kick at their luminous concentration on him. They seemed to be scouring his soul, asking questions he had no answers for. Not yet.

Give me time, he thought, but didn't say the words. They would sound like a promise and he instinctively shied from making any promises. He smiled to smooth over any angst she felt and spoke a truth that held no sense of danger to either of them. 'Just looking at you gives me pleasure.'

Her smile rewarded him, warm sparkles in her eyes softening their dark focus. A daring glint emerged as she answered, 'I would like to look at you but you have too many clothes on.'

He laughed, delighted to oblige her wish, swiftly removing his suitcoat and tossing it on a nearby armchair. 'How are you at undoing bow ties?'

She cocked her head in teasing consideration. 'I think I'm up to the challenge.'

Her hands lifted to the base of his throat and Zack sucked in a quick breath as he felt her fingers go to work, his pulse quickening underneath her touch. He concentrated on removing his cufflinks. His own fingers felt thick and clumsy, impatient to be rid of the task, wanting to roam over her again.

Control, he fiercely recited, but by the time he'd dropped the cufflinks on the table holding the fishbowl, the bowtie was gone, half his shirt buttons were undone, and her hands were gliding over his bare flesh, fingers tracing the taut muscles of his neck and shoulders, raising havoc with his determination to move slowly. He found himself tearing at the remaining buttons, almost ripping the shirt in his haste to get it off.

Her hands were stroking his upper arms as he yanked off the long sleeves and even as the frustrating piece of clothing dropped to the floor, she stepped in and pressed her mouth to the hollow between his shoulder-blades, her hot succulent lips firing up his blood, her hands continuing to stroke down his arms, making the fine hair on them crackle with electricity.

He didn't move, didn't dare to move in case he exploded into action. Besides, he'd wanted to register her affect on him, wanted to understand it, and he'd done this to her, hadn't he, while she stood still? He could stand still, too, and let her touch wash through him, building his awareness of how and why she excited him so much.

Her hands were at his waist now. Every muscle in his body flexed as he imagined them moving to unfasten his trousers. But they didn't. They glided up his rib cage, and her mouth trailed hot sensuous kisses over the breadth of his chest, her teeth lightly tugging on the springy curls at the centre of it, her tongue licking, tasting, and Zack's mind was totally jammed by the sensations shooting through him. Thinking of anything else was not an option.

He'd never considered *his* nipples erotic zones but when she latched onto them, the bolt of excitement was so sharp and intense, his hands instinctively took defensive action, burrowing through the thick curtain of her hair, compulsively intent on pulling her head away until... *Her* hand moved down over the flat of his stomach, making his skin crawl with sensitivity, fingers reaching under the waistband of his trousers, distracting him with her touch on other erogenous areas, and he could feel his erection burgeoning. If she took hold of him...

The need for control snapped into action again. He seized her wrists and lifted her arms to his shoulders, automatically raising her head from his chest where she'd heightened his excitement to an almost intolerable level. He kissed her quickly, his head whirling with the urge to be the dominant force, to take and be taken on his terms.

His tongue punished hers with hard invasive strength, overriding the seductive power of her mouth, yet even her submission was insidiously exciting, conjuring up how it would be when he plunged into her, her hot silky flesh giving way, stretching and compressing voluptuously around him.

He had to stop this or it would be over in a flash. 'Clothes,' he muttered, remembering her wish to look at him.

He stepped back, severing all contact, bumping into the chair he'd tossed his suitcoat on. He leaned against it as he whipped off his shoes and socks. *Go slow,* he raged at himself, taking more time over removing his trousers and briefs, wanting at least a little dignity in getting naked in front of her.

She didn't move. He felt her eyes on him, all over him, and when he finally straightened up, he met her gaze with a challenging pride that denied any self-consciousness in being bared to her sight, though every muscle in his body was taut with intensely male aggression, every nerve strung out from the frustration he'd imposed on himself. He was a man and never had he felt his sexuality more keenly.

Yet the instant he saw her expression—the soft look of wonder on her face, the vulnerable awe in her eyes—he was swept by the urge to be gentle with her, which put him strangely at odds with himself. Most of the women he'd met in recent times were ambitious, manipulative. They didn't draw tenderness from him. It was weird feeling the violent pounding of his heart melt into a muted curl of caring, a different form of desire that was intrinsically linked to *this* woman.

'Now your clothes,' he said, his voice gruff with unaccustomed emotion.

'Yes,' she whispered, a soft breathy agreement that tingled in his ears as he moved around behind her, stepping close enough to effect what he wanted without pressing any physical contact.

He parted her long rippling hair and moved it forward, over her shoulders, baring the nape of her neck and the elegant slope of her upper back, no angular bones, just satin-smooth skin leading down to the strapless red dress.

He unhooked the top fastening of the snugly fitted bodice and slowly drew the zipper down to her waist, exposing the highly feminine indentation of her spine. There was no interruption to it. She wore no bra. And Zack was tempted into stroking his fingers down the intriguing little valley, smiling as the caress raised a convulsive little shiver. She was as sensitised to his touch as he was to hers. Which was only right and immensely satisfying.

The dress gaped further open as he lowered the zipper to its full length, revealing the thin strips of a black G-string circling her fantastically small waist and erotically bisecting the luscious twin globes of her bottom. He'd never seen a sexier sight. It trapped the breath in his lungs and shot stabs of urgency to his groin.

Impatient for a full view of her, he quickly peeled the dress from her hips and it fell to her feet, leaving his hands free to trace every delectable curve, to cup the lush roundness that jutted so provocatively, he had to fight the urge to move forward.

Not yet. Not yet.

He hooked his thumbs under the waistline of her G-string and watched it slide over the soft mounds, down the long lissome thighs. The silky crotch of it caught at her knees. He slid his hand between her legs to release it, the flimsy fabric warm and moist from her inner excitement, bringing his arousal to flashpoint again.

Barely controlling himself, he raked the incredibly sexy garment down the taut curves of her calves and lifted her feet, one by one, sliding off her high-heeled sandals at the same time—all black straps trailing over dark red toenails, another exotic touch that stirred the raging heat in his blood.

The blinding need for action had him hooking an arm under her knees and hoisting her up against his chest as he came upright. He whirled her away from the fishbowl table, his gaze darting, seeking the door to her bedroom, finding it, his legs surging towards it with powerful purpose. It stood ajar, only needing a shove to open it wide enough to let them through to the bed—a double bed covered by a leopard-skin rug with the sheen of velvet, gold satin pillows.

The sheer animal sensuality of it tugged deeply at the most primal instincts in Zack. This was the place. This was the time. This was the woman. And he would not leave until he'd had his fill of her. But he wanted more light, needed to see all of her before plunging into the dark jungle of total intimacy where the beat of their bodies would consume his awareness of anything else.

He spotted a switch by the door, turned it on. Two lamps on either side of her bed—black and gold—spread a warm glow around the room. It looked right, felt right. White light was too harsh. It would have been better with a host of flickering candles—fire burning without and within—but this was a fleeting thought, overtaken by the desire to feast his eyes on all the female lushness now pressed so close to his chest.

He stood her on the bed. The lamplight gleamed on the living curtain of her hair swishing softly over the voluptuous fullness of her breasts, rose-red nipples peeking through the seductive veil, hard and pointed, provoking him into closing his mouth around them, lashing them with his tongue, loving the taste of her arousal, wanting more.

She'd wrapped her arms around his head, holding him to her, but he wouldn't be held. Not yet. He pulled back to take in this incredibly beautiful frontal view of her, to glide his hands over every inch of her, the smoothly fleshed midriff, the narrowness over her waist, the wide cradle of her hips.

His gaze locked onto the neatly trimmed arrow of dark hair, pointing to the cleft between her thighs. Her skin quivered underneath his fingertips as he traced it down and stroked around the apex. He stooped, pressing his face to the tight springy curls, breathing in the musky scent of her desire for him.

It wasn't enough. He scooped her legs out on either side of his and lowered her to the bed, dipping his mouth into the soft lips of her sex, tasting her hot wetness, laving the hidden centre of excitement, a sweetly intimate fondling that arched her body in wild and wanton invitation.

She writhed to the rhythm of his stroking, cried out in frantic pleading, snatched at his hair, fingers scrabbling, curling, tugging, and he exulted in her need for him, pushing it to the edge of shattering before he lifted himself over her.

Instantly her legs locked around him, her hips rocking, urging him forward. Her hands grabbed and plucked at his shoulders, fingernails digging in, dragging. Her hair spilled over the bedcover in a tumultuous tangle and her eyes blazed at him with the animal ferocity of a leopard about to bring down its prey and devour it.

The long-suppressed violence of his own desire burst into action. He seized her hands and slammed them down above her head, determined on being the possessor, not the possessed. He surged into the slick passage to her innermost being and dropped his head to plunder her mouth in a passionate drive to complete his invasion, to glory in his dominant power to take as he wished.

Yet she met him with such a feverish fusion of heat, he lost any sense of separate goals, separate identities, separate lives with separate needs. They were immersed in each other, wildly hungering for every fantastic nuance of being joined. Their mouths clung, feeding on the explosion of sensations that savaged any possible denial of togetherness. Her breasts pressed into his chest, their hardened nipples rubbing his taut muscles with tantalising sweeps.

He automatically released her hands, craving every possible touch, uncaring what she did or how she did it, wanting an absolute twining. They crashed onto his back, pushing and pulling, egging him into a fast series of thrusts that she rolled around in an ecstasy of revelling in the hard heated fullness of him, loving every powerful stroke, arching herself to receive the utmost penetration, clamping around him, moaning with the intense satisfaction of it.

It goaded him into pleasuring her as long as he

could, exulting in her response, feeling like a mountaineer scaling the highest heights and she was drawing him there from peak to peak. His own screaming need demanded a lift in tempo and the last crescendo was his, raising them both to an exquisite cusp of delight before abandoning themselves to the sweet free-fall into blissful peace, wrapped in a togetherness that seeped into his soul and happily resided there.

The rest of the night was spent in a sensual daze of touching, kissing, merging. Zack no longer felt any need for some ascendancy over what they shared. He was awash with all the seductive sensations of intense intimacy, letting it flow as either he or she fancied.

At times he felt his heart swell with the joy of it, his mind float with the wonder of it, and all he ended up identifying was the undeniable fact that Catherine Trent was the source of all these incredible feelings. Whatever made her the woman she was appealed to him on unfathomable levels and he could not have enough of her.

She was his mate on every instinctive level. He knew it to the very marrow of his bones. Yet whether she would mesh with his working life was a question he shied from considering, not wanting this all too brief time with her spoiled by any conflict of interests. It was easier simply to savour the perfection of their deeply mutual desire while it lasted.

In the end, she slipped from the contented languor of satiation into sleep, and still he took immense pleasure in looking at her, stroking her long silky hair, basking in the warmth of her soft breathing, loving the feel of her cuddled close to him. He didn't ask why was it so. It just was. He didn't know if it would always be like this with her. He cared only about now.

There was no place for her in his immediate future which was already mapped out in his mind. When it was time to go he didn't wake her, didn't want to talk, didn't want to say goodbye. Very carefully he slid his body out of contact with hers, watching her settle comfortably without him, though she heaved a sigh that seemed to waft around his heart, silently pleading for him to fill the emptiness again.

For several moments he stood by the bed, torn between the need to go and the desire to stay with her. But there was no choice. He had commitments to fulfil. Catherine knew that. They were here because she hadn't wanted to wake alone in a hotel room—here in the place she called home...with her goldfish.

This last thought brought a smile and eased him out of her bedroom. His clothes were still where he'd left them in the living room. Hers were, too. He nodded to the fish, mentally greeting them—*Hi, Rhett! Hi, Scarlet!*—and grinned as they darted around the bowl to stare at him, their mouths working very energetically as though in a burst of fish chatter that undoubtedly had meaning if only he was a telepath on their wavelength.

Good company, Catherine had said, and he wondered if she made up conversations with them. Happy fish in their Feng Shui bowl. Happiness and harmony…it was what he'd felt with Catherine Trent these past few hours, once his conflict over her power to drive him beyond control had ceased to matter.

As he picked up his clothes and dressed, he pondered the quandary she represented. She did have power over him, an addictive power that made him wary of establishing her in his life. A relationship meant constant ties, limitations to his freedom to be wherever he had to be to fulfil his contractual obligations. Would she drop everything to come with him, be with him?

Unlikely.

It was too much to ask anyway. Women had the right to their own lives, their own careers, and he'd seen what long separations did to relationships in the movie world. Better to leave Catherine to her own work and friends and family.

He finished dressing and looked wryly at Rhett and Scarlet. Catherine couldn't pack goldfish in a suitcase. This was her home and Zack knew he didn't belong here.

He turned to go.

On the floor in front of the armchair lay the dark red rose he'd taken from her hair. He remembered having tucked it into his breast pocket. It must have tipped out when he'd tossed the coat on the chair. He bent and picked it up, meaning to set it on the table by the fishbowl.

It was an artificial rose, perfect, reminding him of many things about Catherine and how he'd felt with her. He twirled it around in his fingers, telling himself it was stupid to keep such a memento. Yet he still held *her* rose as he walked to the door, released the safety chain and let himself out.

He had no idea what he'd do with it.

He just wanted it.

CHAPTER NINE

CATHERINE saw the sparkling excitement in her sister's vivid blue eyes and knew what she was going to say even as Livvy leaned over the table to deliver her news in a confidential whisper.

'I'm pregnant.'

So am I.

The words almost spilled out, the desire to share welling up in a rush. Catherine only just clamped down on them, realising the revelation would totally goggle her sister's happy eyes and switch the focus of this get-together onto her, which would be grossly unfair. This was Livvy's moment in the sun and she certainly didn't deserve to have any uneasy shadows falling over it.

Catherine stretched her treacherous mouth into a delighted grin. 'Congratulations! I'm very happy for you and Pete.'

Livvy sat back, clapping her hands in sheer joy as she crowed, 'And just two months after our wedding!'

They'd be having babies together, Catherine thought in black irony. The difference was Livvy had done everything right—married the man she loved, a man who wanted children with her—while she...

'I thought it might take ages since I've been on the pill for so long,' Livvy rushed on.

It took only one night.

Her sister's eyes twinkled wickedly. 'I think Pete must be very potent. Besides which, we've certainly been giving it every chance.'

And she had told Zack it was safe.

'Well, good for you,' Catherine said with as much warmth as she could muster.

'I couldn't wait to tell you,' Livvy bubbled. 'I only found out this morning. So that's why I rang you at work and insisted you meet me for this afternoon tea. You see? It *is* important family business.'

'Very important,' Catherine echoed, and she'd worked through her lunch hour to fit in with Livvy's cavalier command to take time off in order to drive from Botany to Circular Quay and meet her at the Intercontinental Hotel for this private get-together. Her boss wasn't keen on employees skipping out early and Catherine needed her boss to be onside when she was finally forced to confess to single motherhood.

'Pete will be joining us here for drinks after he's finished work. He's just as excited as I am. But I wanted to tell you first.'

'What about Mum and Dad?'

Who were bound to be disappointed in her for getting herself into this situation. Much less stress to stay silent as long as she could.

'We're dropping over to their place tonight, after Pete and I have a celebratory dinner.'

'Better not drink too much then.'

'Only a glass or two of champagne. Ah...' Livvy smiled up at the waiter who had arrived at their table to serve them. 'Our cappuccinos. I ordered for you, Catherine, since you were late arriving.'

And she always had a cappuccino…except she'd gone off coffee, preferring a sweet cup of tea which seemed to settle the queaziness she felt most mornings. Still, at this time of day one cappuccino should be manageable. Unfortunately Livvy had also ordered cream cakes and rich pastries that curdled Catherine's stomach just looking at them. Cucumber sandwiches would have been infinitely preferable.

They did serve elegant afternoon teas here in The Cortile, a huge two-storeyed area that had once been part of the old treasury building, now incorporated in this very classy hotel. The colonnaded walkways running around it gave it a leisurely atmosphere, as did the cane armchairs in which they sat, and the grand piano being played by an excellent pianist, providing pleasant background music. It should have been very relaxing and would have been if Catherine didn't have to guard her tongue.

'No morning sickness yet?' she asked once the waiter had gone.

Livvy laughed and shook her head. 'I guess that's in front of me. I'll have to buy some books and read up on all the dos and don'ts.' She gave Catherine an arch look. 'Now if you were a proper older sister, you'd be able to advise me on all this. Still no man on your horizon?'

Pain stabbed her heart. There'd been no contact from Zack since the night of the wedding. He hadn't even woken her to say goodbye.

Gone with the wind…

She gave her sister a droll look of exasperation to cover up the wretched emptiness in her soul. 'You asked me here to talk happy talk so let's concentrate on you and your baby. Do you fancy a son or a daughter?'

'One of each would be lovely.'

'Twins?'

Livvy laughed. 'I hope not. Just one at a time but in any order. Boy or girl…it doesn't matter.'

Such blissful carefree plans.

A mountainous wave of envy hit Catherine and she struggled to fight through it as her younger sister rattled on about her ideal family. It wasn't Livvy's fault that her own life was in such a mess. She seemed to get herself embroiled in one bad choice after another; holding on to Stuart Carstairs when he wasn't worth holding on to, and now Zack…had she no *sense* of when to let go? Did fantasy have a bigger grip on her than reality?

The morning after Zack had left, she had lain in the bed he had shared, overwhelmingly aware of the empty place beside her, feeling bereft and miserably alone, telling herself she should get up and go to a pharmacy, purchase the pill that would keep her *safe*. It was the sensible thing to do.

Except she'd turned thirty-two this past year, and she couldn't imagine falling in love with another man or accepting second best just to get married and have a family. If she was ever to have a child, she *wanted* Zack Freeman to be the father.

She hadn't actually decided to get pregnant by him, and there'd been no certainty whatsoever about having conceived—women of her age often took months of trying before falling pregnant. She'd simply kept dallying with the idea that it might have happened—could happen—if she did nothing.

None of this had been really *real* to her then. More a romantic fantasy. And the more she'd thought about it, the less inclined she'd been to wilfully take away the possibility that a new life had been created in the heat of her night with Zack—a life she would love and cherish—a part of him she would always have.

She'd left the decision to Fate.

If it was meant to be, it was meant to be.

Not for one moment had she thought the consequences through or considered the practicalities of her situation if she was faced with being a single mother. Reality had only begun to bite when the pregnancy test showed positive. In the past few weeks, more and more frightening realities had been creeping up on her and she didn't know how to handle any of them.

Here was Livvy, chatting on about how she intended to keep working until she was six months into her pregnancy, then put in her resignation because she wanted to be a full-time mother, especially since she and Pete planned to have their babies in reasonably close succession. No worries about ready support for her family dream. Pete was a dependable bread-winner and dying to take on the fatherhood role.

Whereas Zack…

Her stomach cramped. If she dared to contact him

and confess her pregnancy, he'd probably hate her for it, believing she had deliberately deceived him, trapped him into fatherhood. Her mind shied from even considering taking such a step.

Quite clearly Zack had not wanted to risk having a child. She couldn't imagine he'd want a lifelong responsibility loaded onto his shoulders when he hadn't agreed to it. So it was impossible to ask for any child support from him. She had to go it alone.

And she would. Because now that the pregnancy was real, she fiercely wanted this baby, regardless of the difficulties and hardships ahead of her. The need for it was as deeply primitive as the feelings Zack had stirred in her.

More so.

Zack wasn't hers to keep but their child was. If nothing else, she'd have this, and already her love for the life she now carried burned in her heart like a beacon that she knew would shine over any dark days she experienced.

It wasn't the joy Livvy was feeling.

It was a passion.

Maybe that was the difference between their two natures.

Livvy was a straight-line kind of person while she was driven by highs and lows. Her sister was never going to understand any of the choices she'd made, especially those relating to Zack. It was definitely best to keep it all to herself until she couldn't any longer.

'Catherine, you haven't eaten anything and your coffee must be cold by now,' Livvy pointed out.

'It's all too rich for me, Livvy,' she excused. 'I'm sure Pete will help you out with it when he comes.' She quickly picked up her cup… 'Still warm.' …and sipped before smiling to assure her sister all was well.

'Don't tell me you're dieting.' It was a castigating comment.

'No. But I did have a late lunch,' Catherine lied, hating the necessity to lie, yet needing to excuse her lack of appetite so her sister wouldn't go on and on about it. 'I just don't feel like eating anymore. Sorry…'

Livvy shrugged and helped herself to a second pastry. 'I feel hungry all the time. Must be my hormones getting out of balance or something.'

Again her sister rattled on, leaving Catherine to wonder how many lies she would end up telling. Deceit did not sit comfortably with her. Better to avoid meetings like this until she was ready to confront everyone with the truth.

It was a relief when Pete arrived, lifting the onus of a one-on-one conversation with Livvy. Though again Catherine found herself wracked with envy at the love so openly expressed between her sister and brother-in-law in their greeting and manner to each other.

Worse was their mutual exhilaration in having a baby on the way. Livvy preened as Pete fussed over her, adoring the mother of his child, only too eager to watch over her every comfort and carry out her every pleasure.

So it should be, Catherine savagely told herself,

and if that was not her lot it was because of the choices she'd made and it was now up to her to get used to not having the whole rosy package. Glasses of champagne were ordered and brought to their table. She forced herself to make appropriate toasts, to smile and laugh in all the right places, and was doing fine until Pete brought up Zack's name.

'Hey! Did you hear the news about Zack?' he tossed out, grinning from ear to ear.

She shook her head, not trusting herself to speak in a tone of mild interest.

'He won the BAFTA award for Special Visual Effects in London last night. It was in the newspaper this morning. He's really scooping the pool this year. The film he worked on scored Best Picture Drama in the Golden Globes. Only the Academy Award to go.'

'He's bound to win it,' Livvy chimed in. 'You know, Pete, given the big rush of what's happening for him, it was really good of Zack to drop everything and come to our wedding.'

'Sure was,' he agreed.

Catherine loosened her throat enough to ask, 'Have you heard from him since then?'

'No. Don't expect to until he lands back home,' came the matter-of-fact reply.

'I thought…as old friends…'

'We'll chew over it all when we meet up again.' Pete grinned. 'It's only women who can't wait to share everything over the phone.'

Livvy laughed and playfully punched him on the arm. 'You're not to go ga-ga over the phone bill again.'

'It was only the shock of it, sweetheart. I'll be expecting it next time and won't even blink. Promise.'

'So, are you expecting Zack back in Australia soon?' Catherine pressed, unable to leave the subject alone, craving some personal news of him or a reason to hope…

Pete shrugged. 'The way things are lining up for him, it would only be a flying visit when and if he comes. Like for the wedding. In and out.'

He'd been in and out her life twice. No promises for a third time, yet with Pete now married to her sister, another connection might happen. If it was months from now and he visited Pete, he could well find out his old friend's sister-in-law was pregnant. A year on and he could hear she'd had a child. Would he put two and two together? And then what?

If he ignored the news, then there was no hope of any future with him. Yet if he came to her… Catherine's heart began to quiver at that possibility. His child…would he feel he had to offer financial support? Take up visiting rights? The future was suddenly a minefield that could explode in her face if Zack took a terrible negative attitude towards her for what she'd done.

'Catherine…'

Livvy was eyeing her with concern, a slight frown drawing her brows together. It jolted Catherine into smoothing out her own expression, hiding any stress she might have inadvertently shown.

'Sorry…wool-gathering. Did I miss something?' she asked brightly.

'No.' Livvy grimaced. 'You just looked a bit lonely and lost. It made me think...'

'Livvy, I'm tired. It was a hard day at work and I think the champagne's gone to my head. If you and Pete don't mind, I'll head off home now and leave you to celebrate together.' She started to rise from her chair.

'No...wait! I need to say this.' Determined purpose in her sister's voice.

Stifling a frustrated sigh, Catherine sank onto the cushioned seat again, hoping not to be held up much longer. Her nerves were frayed from keeping up a happy facade. 'What's so pressing?' she asked, trying for a note of indulgence.

'Maybe I did wrong by you last year,' came the worried reply.

Catherine looked blankly at her, desperately hiding her inner churning. If Livvy brought up the blind date with Zack...

'I truly believed Stuart Carstairs was bad for you, but that was your business and I shouldn't have interfered, telling you stuff you didn't want to hear.'

Catherine held her breath, not knowing where this was leading.

'I guess everyone's different,' Livvy mused. 'Maybe we don't get to pick whom we love. They just complement something in us...' She sighed. 'Anyhow, I just want to say if there's any chance of you getting back with Stuart, don't let my opinion stop you. I had no right to...'

'Stuart?' The name burst from Catherine in almost

hysterical relief. 'There's no way in the world I'd ever want to get back with Stuart Carstairs.'

'No?'

'No!'

'Then why haven't you...? I mean, you've shown no interest in anyone else and I thought... Who am I to judge what suits you best?'

Catherine summoned up a rueful smile. 'Not Stuart, I promise you. Stop worrying about me, Livvy. I'll make my own way.' She pushed onto her feet again, shaking her head fondly at the newly wed couple. 'Be happy for you. I am.'

This time she made good her escape.

She collected her car from the opera house car park and with the evening peak-hour traffic well and truly over, it was a hassle-free drive home to Randwick. It felt good to close her apartment door and shut the rest of the world out.

She walked across the living room to the goldfish bowl and smiled at Rhett and Scarlet who were responding eagerly to her presence. She didn't have to hide anything from them. They gave her pleasure and made no demands...except for food. It cost her very little to supply that.

A baby would cost a great deal more, on many levels. But whatever the price she would pay it...somehow. She would never, never ask Zack for anything. She'd taken the gift of a child from him. He owed her nothing. But the child was not all hers. The big question was...how would he react to it?

The telephone rang, drawing her over to the kitchen counter. Any distraction from her thoughts was welcome. She didn't speculate on who might be calling. She simply picked up the receiver and gave her name. There was a moment of silence then her name was repeated at the other end of the line.

'Catherine…'

The deep timbre of the voice was instantly recognisable, stopping her heart dead and sending prickles down her spine.

'…it's Zack Freeman.'

The confirmation did nothing to loosen her tongue which was stuck to the roof of her mouth. The shock of hearing from him held her utterly frozen.

'I was wondering if you could get a goldfish-sitter?'

The crazy question jolted her into croaking, 'What?'

'Someone to look after Rhett and Scarlet if you flew to L.A. for a week.'

'L.A.?' She knew she was sounding stupid but couldn't snap herself out of the stunned daze.

'I would like very much if you'd partner me to the Academy Awards ceremony.'

Partner him!

'When?' The question tripped off her tongue.

'It would mean flying from Sydney on Thursday, twenty-first of March. I'll book the flight and you can pick up the E-ticket at the Qantas desk. You'll be met at LAX airport by a chauffeur and transported to the Regent Beverley Wiltshire Hotel where I have a suite booked. All you have to do is arrange for time off work and find someone to look after the goldfish.'

The Regent Beverley Wiltshire—it was where they'd made the movie *Pretty Woman*. Was she to be Zack's *pretty woman* for his big Hollywood night?

'Catherine...will you come?'

She should have asked, *why her?* She should have asked dozens of questions. But a wild rush of blood to the head blotted out all of them.

'Yes,' she said.

'Good!' A wealth of satisfaction in his voice. 'Call Qantas tomorrow and they'll give you the details.'

'Zack...'

'Mmm?'

Nothing. She'd just wanted to say his name. 'I'll look forward to seeing you again,' she rushed out.

'I want you with me,' he simply stated.

And that was the end of it.

Or the beginning of something Catherine hadn't dared to count on.

It was the end of February now. Three, four weeks...hopefully she still wouldn't be showing her pregnancy. Whether she would tell him or not depended on...too much for her to even contemplate. She would just go. Whatever happened with Zack Freeman in Los Angeles would make the decision for her.

CHAPTER TEN

SHE was in bed and fast asleep, just as he'd left her three months ago, her glorious hair strewn across the pillows, the seductive curves of her lush body outlined by the sheet that covered her. Catherine...

He didn't say her name out loud but it rolled through his mind, filling it with pleasure, and all the doubts he'd nursed since calling her to come suddenly seemed totally irrelevant. She was here. And so was he. It felt good...right.

He moved swiftly to the bathroom, stripped off, got under the shower to freshen himself up after his flight from New York. It was just past two in the afternoon. The desk clerk had told him Catherine had arrived at seven this morning. She was probably trying to sleep off jetlag. It was a killer trip from Sydney to L.A.

As the water sprayed him in an invigorating burst, he shook his head over the London model who'd accompanied him to the BAFTA awards in the U.K. That woman hadn't known when to stop posing, courting every photographer in sight, puckering up to him as though they were an item, loving all the limelight, thinking she was irresistibly sexy despite her skinny figure and not having half the natural beauty Catherine had. He'd ended up hating her high screechy voice, hating her busy hands, hating her empty name-dropping chatter.

One night with that female egomaniac and the impulse to call the only woman he really wanted had been too strong to deny. The sweet relief of hearing her simple *yes*—no scatty questions, no fluffing around, no irritating drama, just *yes*—had put a smile on his face for days afterwards. He just hoped she hadn't been reading more into this invitation than there was. A week with her was all he could fit in.

But what a week it was going to be!

Catherine…his heart seemed to lift with the lovely rhythm of her name.

He was grinning as he towelled himself dry, the excitement of having her here, waiting for him in the next room, was like a fizzy cocktail running through his blood. He strode back to the bed. She hadn't stirred. The need to touch, to awaken an awareness of him would not wait. He lifted the sheet and slid his body down beside hers, propping himself up on one elbow, wanting to watch for the first flicker of her long eyelashes.

With featherlight fingertips he stroked the wavy hair away from her beautiful face. No make-up, he noticed. She needed none. The fine texture of her skin had no blemishes. Her lips, provocatively pouting in the relaxed state of sleep, were a rosy-brown colour. And he knew her eyes had their own unique attraction that no artifice could improve upon.

He trailed his fingers down the soft curve of her cheek, then slowly traced her full lower lip. Her tongue licked out, instinctively seeking to reduce the sensitivity he'd aroused. A slight crease appeared between her eyes, disturbance at a subconscious level. He was smiling when her lashes lifted, a delicate shift then a sharp flick open, as though consciousness had come in a rush.

'Hi!' he said, happy to greet her into his life again.

'Hi!' she responded with a sigh that spread into a slow sensual smile, and he saw the amber irises warm to gold, welcoming him back into her life.

'Good of you to come.'

'Good of you to ask me.'

He laughed, delighted by her laid-back attitude. 'An act of total selfishness, I'm afraid.'

'Oh, I don't know. Seems to me there's quite a bit of giving in it. The first-class seat on the flight was much appreciated. The limousine made me feel like a VIP. And this suite…' She gave him an anxious look. 'Please tell me it's some kind of perk related to your work.'

Her concern over the cost amused him. Other women he knew would take this for granted. 'Definitely a perk related to my work,' he assured her and it wasn't a complete lie. He was raking in millions from the film that was winning him awards—a percentage deal—and he could well afford this extravagance. Besides, the trappings of success was a power tool in Hollywood. He'd be inviting people here—business under the guise of parties.

'The penthouse suite,' she breathed in awe, rolling her eyes. 'I almost died when I was shown into it.'

'Is that why you're in bed?' he teased.

'I thought it had to be a dream and when I woke

up...' She reached up and touched his face. 'This *is* real, isn't it?'

'It feels real to me.'

He leaned over her, brushing her lips with his, tasting them with light flicks of his tongue. Her arms wound around his neck, inviting more *reality,* and Zack was only too ready to oblige, to reacquaint himself with the whole intensely desirable package of Catherine Trent.

His hands skimmed her beautiful body with possessive eagerness as he deepened the kiss, igniting the passion that flared so quickly between them. Her breasts felt firmer than he'd remembered, her waist less emphatically indented. Probably carrying a bit more weight, he thought, and dismissed the minor physical changes, loving the feel of her anyway, the lush curves, the softness of her flesh, the silky smoothness of her skin.

It was so easy to immerse himself in her. She was instantly receptive, as hot for him as he was for her, shuddering with pleasure as he sank into her creamy depths, locking her legs around him to hold on to the intensely satisfying intimacy, kissing with a hunger that matched his. They fitted in every sense, and he exulted in this perfect union, wallowed in it, drove it to as many heights as he could manage before totally expending himself.

'Now that was better than good,' he said when he'd recovered breath enough to speak.

'Mmm...' she purred against his chest.

'You're not to go back to sleep, Catherine.'

'Just making sure you're real,' she mumbled, gliding a hand towards his groin.

'Believe it.'

He grabbed her seductive hand and pressed it over his heart, which was still thumping at an accelerated rate, very much alive and kicking. However, the practical reality was she needed to get out and do some walking after her long flight or her body clock would never catch up to L.A. time. As much as he was tempted to stay right where he was all afternoon, it wouldn't be good for her. Besides which, he could completely sate himself with her tonight. He had a whole week of nights to do what he wanted.

'Have you been to L.A. before, Catherine?'

'No. First time.'

'And you haven't moved from this suite since you arrived?'

'I was waiting for you.'

'Well, now that I'm here, I'll take you out for some sight-seeing. We'll go to Santa Monica, walk down the mall, pick up something to eat, watch the buskers, look at the stalls. Maybe stroll along the beach.' He grinned as he recalled their first night together at Spoon Bay. She *was* like a siren from the sea, still calling to him. Even her pets were fish. He wound his other hand through her hair and lightly tugged, feeling the tide of desire rising again and knowing he should stave it off. 'Okay with you?'

She levered herself up to smile happy agreement at him. 'Now that you mention it, I am hungry.'

'Want something to eat first?'

'No. I'd rather go out.'

'Then let's get dressed and go.'

She rolled off the bed, picked up a bathrobe and had it on before he could really savour the sight of her naked. But then her arm lifted and hoisted the rippling mass of her hair out from under the collar and he enjoyed watching the long silky tresses float around her shoulders as she headed for the bathroom.

Catherine.... Catherine Trent.

He was fully aroused again. Control was almost a lost cause around her. Cold shower, he dictated, and no looking at her until she presented herself fully dressed. There were three bedrooms and four bathrooms in this suite. He took himself off to the bedroom where he'd directed his luggage be dropped and enforced the necessary discipline, although there was no suppressing the zing of anticipation in his blood.

There was no other woman like her.

Not in his experience.

Maybe spending a week with her would diminish the addictive power she had over him, show him she wasn't so attractive when it came to mixing in other areas of his life. What little time they'd spent together had been hyper-time, intensely sexual. He needed to slow that down, explore more of her, get some all-encompassing perspective that would let him feel free to move on from here.

That was a reasonable plan of action.

But as he forced himself to move out into the living room and plant himself in front of the floor-to-ceiling windows, which gave a magnificent view of the skyline, he could barely bring himself to wait until she appeared.

Catherine was on tenterhooks that Zack might follow her into the bathroom. Her heart was galloping at the prospect, frightened that he would notice the thickening of her waist, which she could do nothing to disguise. He hadn't commented on it in bed, but touch was different to sight and they'd both been caught up in the urgent need for intimate connection.

She beat all speed records under the shower and wrapped herself in the bathrobe again before returning to the bedroom to dress. It was a huge relief to find Zack gone from it, but aware that he was somewhere in the suite and could re-join her at any moment, she wasted no time in choosing what to wear. Walking, he'd said. Her black stretch jeans, matching battle jacket, the red top that skimmed rather than hugged her waist, and Reeboks on her feet—that should take her anywhere with reasonable style and comfort.

Once fully dressed, she relaxed enough to take some time over her hair and a bit of make-up. There was no telling whom they might meet and she wanted Zack to feel proud of her. Fortunately the sleep had done her good. She was no longer feeling like death warmed up, as she had after the long flight, and the queaziness had left her stomach.

But what about tomorrow morning? she asked herself as she brushed the tangles out of her hair. How long could she keep deceiving Zack about her pregnancy? More to the point, did she want to? Apart from subjecting herself to the panic that had just churned through her, she wasn't ever going to feel *right* while she kept this secret from him. She could feel herself tensing up at the thought of the next few hours in his company, pretending she had nothing to worry about.

But if she didn't pretend...this was her first real chance to relate to him on other levels beside the sexual, her first chance to see how much he was drawn to her as *a person,* not just as a *pretty woman* on hand in his penthouse suite. If she blurted out she was pregnant and told him he'd fathered the baby, she was frightened of precipitating a crisis that would shatter any hopeful harmony she might reach with him, given a few days together.

Satisfied with her appearance, Catherine took several deep breaths to calm her jumpy nerves, then walked out to the amazing living room, telling herself not to be overawed by all this spacious luxury. Only Zack's response to her counted, not the glamorous surroundings nor what they signalled about how big a success he was in his world. What lay in his heart...that was what she had to learn while she was here.

The suite was on the top floor of the Beverly Wing with a wrap-around balcony on three sides. Zack stood by one of the floor-to-ceiling windows, gazing out. He had an imperious look about him, the proud cast of his head, the tall, powerful physique, clothed in black jeans and leather jacket. Catherine wondered if he had more worlds to conquer in his mind, or would he feel satisfied with reaching the zenith of this one…an Academy Award…the Hollywood dream?

'Zack…' she called, wanting him to turn to her.

He snapped around, exuding an animal vitality that instantly said he would always have more places to go. There would never be resting on any laurels for Zack Freeman.

'Ready…' he said with relish, his eyes eating her up from head to toe with more than warm approval.

He closed the distance between them with a few quick strides. The magnetic energy targeting her held Catherine breathless and tingling and when Zack hooked her arm around his with purposeful possessiveness, her heart swelled with the wild hope that he wouldn't want to let her go. Not this time.

'I've called for a car. You'll like Santa Monica. It's fun,' he informed her.

And so it proved to be. A whole street was blocked to traffic, an open mall where the most amazingly colourful people strolled along, wearing way-out clothes and incredible hairdos. A jazz band was selling soul at one end of it. At the other was a string quartet offering classical music. There were buskers in between, offering other forms of entertainment, like the balloon blower who created plastic animals for the children. Restaurants with hugely varied cuisines extended out onto the pavements. Street stalls sold a fascinating array of fashion accessories.

A display of wonderful hats tempted Catherine into trying some on. Zack happily encouraged her, offering critical comment on how well or not each one suited her, enjoying the role of arbiter. A soft reversible hat caught her eye. It felt like velvet and it could be worn as mainly black with a turned up tiger-print rim or the other way around.

'Yes, that one!' Zack said emphatically when she modelled it for him.

'Why this one?' She liked it but didn't see it as extra special.

'Because it's you,' he declared without a moment's hesitation.

'Me?'

'Leopard, tiger…a powerful cat. Beautiful, graceful, lethal.'

She was stunned by this description. 'Is that how you see me?'

He cocked his head in teasing consideration. 'Lethal might be overstating it. Definitely dangerous.'

'A cat?' She looked her incredulity. 'Have I ever shown you claws?'

His smile was very wry. 'You keep digging into my mind, Catherine Trent.'

What about your heart?

She returned the smile. 'You do quite a bit of that to me, Zack Freeman.'

'Good! I'd hate to think you had all the power.'

She shook her head, never having thought she had any power, but his admission did indicate there was more than just physical lust on his side. He thought about her. But was it anywhere as much as she thought about him?

'We'll take this hat,' he said, turning to the salesman and whipping out a twenty dollar note while Catherine was still bemused by his responses.

'I'll pay for it,' she protested.

'It's done.' He grinned as he took her arm and led her on. 'You look great in it.'

'Thank you.' It was still on her head. She left it there. 'My goldfish wouldn't like me as a cat,' she dryly observed.

He laughed. 'They don't get to stroke you and hear you purr.'

The simmering look in his eyes sent a wave of heat through Catherine. The desire he stirred flared between them, choking off any further banter.

'Let's choose a place to eat,' Zack said gruffly, steering her towards the closest restaurant.

Neither of them attempted conversation until they were safely seated with a table between them. Catherine found herself fixating on Zack's hands as he perused a menu, thinking of how seductively his long sensual fingers teased and caressed and aroused. She had to tear her gaze off them and concentrate on ordering a meal. She was hungry, desperately hungry for many things beside food.

When Zack stroked her stomach, would their baby feel his touch as she did, deep in her womb? Would he love it if he knew it was there? Would he come to love her? She needed so much from this week with him.

The waiter came to take their orders. Catherine decided on what she hoped was a bland chicken dish, not wanting anything to upset her stomach tonight. Zack ordered steak and a bottle of wine, which she knew she wouldn't share. Maybe a glass of it wouldn't hurt, but she was glad water was served without her even asking for it.

After the waiter had gone, Zack sat back and eyed her with a rueful twinkle. 'I really want to race you back to the hotel. Why do you suppose you have this effect on me?'

It was another chance to probe his feelings and Catherine seized it. 'Livvy says…maybe we don't get to pick whom we love. They just complement something in us.'

'Love…' Zack frowned over the word, a dark rejection of it in his eyes as he tersely asked, 'You've discussed me with your sister?'

'No, I consider what we've had together very private,' she said slowly, the urge to hurt him as he'd just hurt her welling from the cramp in her heart. 'She was trying to explain away my attachment to another man. A guy she doesn't particularly like.'

The frown deepened over a savage glower. 'You're here with me, being unfaithful to some other guy?'

He certainly didn't like that idea but whether it was jealousy or contempt for such behaviour she wasn't quite sure. 'No. That relationship was over before I ever met you, Zack.' She gave him an ironic smile as she delivered the truth. 'In fact, there hasn't been anyone else since I met you. I haven't *wanted* anyone else.'

Her eyes blazed a challenge. She'd laid out his effect on her. Let him speak now. For several long nerve-racking moments he seemed to weigh what she'd said, then to her intense disappointment, the waiter arrived with the bottle of wine, breaking up the intimate flow between them.

After the wine had been poured and they were left alone again, Zack changed the subject, casually asking, 'So how are Pete and Livvy? Still blissful newlyweds?'

'Very blissful,' Catherine almost snapped, then bluntly stated, 'They're expecting a baby.'

His eyebrows rose in surprise. 'Straight off?'

'It's what they both want.'

'Well, good luck to them.' His mouth twitched into a whimsical little smile. 'Pete will make a very proud Dad.'

The highly sensitive question shot out before she could stop it. 'Do you ever think of having children yourself, Zack?'

He shrugged. 'One day.' He picked up his glass of wine and swirled it around, watching the movement of the liquid, not looking at her. *Deliberately* not looking at her?

Tell him, her mind screamed. *Cut through all this and lay it on the line.*

'Pete's father is a good dad,' Zack remarked musingly. 'He always let his children be. Pete will be like that, too.' His gaze snapped to hers, hard and searing. 'My father wanted to order my life as he saw fit. I had to fight against his edicts all through my teenage years. I wouldn't let him own me. No one owns me.'

Her heart sank.

Freedom was like a religion to him, the zeal for it in his eyes telling her he would never be tied down

by anyone. Unless he chose it. And he'd been given
no choice over her pregnancy.

The scream in her mind dropped to a wail of despair. She said nothing. She picked up her glass of
wine and sipped it, barely stopping herself from grimacing over its sour taste.

'He died when I was twenty-one,' Zack went on.
'For me it was a release. For my mother, too, I think.
No more conflict.'

If he'd witnessed a difficult marriage all through
his childhood, what hope was there of him wanting
marriage at all?

'I guess I'm lucky,' she muttered. 'My parents really do love each other and Livvy and I have always
felt their warm caring for us. We're a very close-knit
family.'

'Yet you live apart from them,' he pointed out.

'I think every adult has a right to their own space.
That doesn't mean the connection isn't there to be
touched whenever it's wanted or needed.'

'Yes.'

Satisfaction glinted in his eyes and Catherine realised she'd just described what he fancied with her—
a connection when the desire for it occurred.

But that wasn't how it was with a baby…a child.
She felt sick.

Their food arrived and she picked at it, feeling
sicker and sicker. Her womb ached, as though it, too,
was being drained of hope. Eventually she had to
excuse herself and head for the ladies' room.
Something was wrong, too wrong for her to ignore.
Her hands were trembling as she locked herself in a

cubicle. A few fumbling moments later she understood what she'd been feeling and her heart was gripped by a wrenching fear.

She was bleeding.

CHAPTER ELEVEN

ZACK put down his knife and fork, giving up on the half-eaten steak. He'd been forcing himself to eat it, any appetite he'd had completely killed by the guilt he felt at having *used* Catherine to satisfy himself. He hadn't promised her anything, hadn't led her to believe in a continuing relationship, but...telling him there hadn't been any other man...talking of *love*... even *children*.

It was obvious now that she'd come to L.A. hoping for something more from him than a protracted tumble in bed, and he'd just swept that mat out from under her feet with brutal efficiency. Which had hurt her. Hurt badly. The meal on her plate was barely touched. She'd looked sick when she'd left the table and she'd been gone now...what? Five, ten minutes? He hoped she wasn't crying.

His chest tightened at the thought of causing her to shed tears. Damn it! He'd meant to deliver a warning, not completely gut her. She'd been so... *accepting* of the situation on their previous two times together. He'd thought...no harm done. Just pleasure on both sides. But that clearly wasn't the case at all.

Not even for him, he thought with savage self-mockery. No other woman had got to him since Catherine. He'd tried to put her out of his mind, dating women who'd be considered prizes by most men, but they'd all left him cold in the end. He knew exactly what Catherine meant. Nothing else measured up to *their* experience. And the bottom line was, he didn't want to give it up.

So what to do now? Apologise? Explain his position? What if she came back to the table and ended it right here? Walked away from him without so much as a backward glance? How would he feel?

Zack didn't have time to analyse the impact such an action would have on him. Catherine *was* on her way back, a set determination on her face and not the slightest bit of warmth or pleasure in her eyes. She didn't move to sit on her chair. She remained standing by the table, a bleak decision in the eyes that met his with unwavering resolution.

Zack found himself rising to his feet, bracing himself for action, adrenalin shooting through his blood at the instinctive urge to fight. 'What is it?' he rapped out, forcing the issue, wanting to deal with it.

'I need your help, Zack.' A flat, bare statement.

'Whatever I can do,' he promised quickly, not having anticipated an appeal for help.

'I don't know anyone here except you. I don't know where to go or what to do. Please…you must help, no matter how you feel about it.'

Her voice cracked over the entreaty and despair welled into a film over her eyes. Alarmed by her intense distress, Zack automatically reached out and closed his hands reassuringly around her shoulders, which were held too stiffly. 'I'm here for you,' he strongly asserted. 'Tell me how I can help.'

'I'm pregnant. I'm bleeding. I think I'm having a miscarriage.'

Three body blows that took his breath away, blew his mind, and contracted every muscle in his body.

'I have to get to a hospital. I don't even know one in Los Angeles. And I'm frightened of...of passing out.'

He fought off the shock. She looked like death. He had to act and act fast.

'Sit down until I get the information we need,' he commanded, forcibly seating her on the chair she'd vacated. His mind zapped into overdrive as he whipped out his mobile telephone from the pocket of his leather jacket. The hotel would have the contacts. Money would buy the quickest and best treatment. He kept his brain clear to make the necessary moves. Time for questions later.

Once Zack took charge, everything passed in a blur to Catherine. While one part of her mind recognised and was intensely grateful for his efficient participation in getting her to emergency treatment, another part shut him out, focusing entirely on keeping still, keeping calm, willing her baby to hold on.

There were questions to be answered when she arrived at the hospital, distracting forms to be filled out. She hadn't thought to take out medical insurance for this trip. Zack stepped in and cut through the red tape, insisting he would take care of everything. Which didn't feel right but she didn't have the energy to argue. She needed all of it to concentrate on holding the fear at bay and doing whatever she could to keep her baby safe.

A doctor examined her. She hadn't lost the baby yet. It was still there. She was to rest quietly tonight and they'd run a scan on her tomorrow to check the situation. A nurse introduced herself and explained the hospital system, showed the button to press if she required attention, saw to all her immediate needs. Finally she was left alone to sleep the night away.

Except she wasn't alone. Zack was still with her in the private room he had arranged. He'd supervised everything, remaining on hand to facilitate whatever he could. He was sitting on a chair beside her bed, and now there was no more to be done, Catherine could no longer shut his presence out of her mind.

He hadn't asked her any questions.

She didn't want to answer any. No point. He'd made his position clear. Marriage and children were not on his agenda. What had been—a week of pleasure with her—had now lost all viability. To his credit, he had risen to her desperate appeal for help, despite the shock it must have been to him, and it was up to her now to cut him free of an involvement that was totally devoid of pleasure.

'Thank you, Zack,' she said quietly, forcing herself to look at him face to face. He deserved that acknowledgment for all he'd done, though it pained her to see the darkly clouded eyes of the man on whom she'd pinned so many futile hopes. 'Please don't feel you have to stay,' she went on. 'I'll manage on my own now.'

The cloud instantly lifted. The sharply penetrating

look he gave her pierced Catherine's soul. 'It's my child, isn't it,' he stated more than asked. No doubt in his mind.

There was no denying it, no evading it. He'd heard her tell the medical staff she was three months' pregnant. 'Yes,' she said flatly, then gathered breath enough to add, 'I lied to you. It wasn't safe. So it's not your fault, Zack. I'm the only one who's responsible for this child.'

That let him off the hook. He could go with a clear conscience. It hadn't been an accident. There'd been no failure of any contraceptive device. This outcome could be directly attributed to a choice she had made—a choice she'd been prepared to live by. Without him.

She half expected a tirade of accusation but it didn't come. Even so, the long drawn-out silence stretched her nerves.

'Did you *want* to fall pregnant, Catherine?'

His voice was carefully void of any criticism. Yet she read into the question the suggestion she'd planned to trap him into fatherhood and she couldn't bear him to think that of her.

'I just wanted *you* that night, Zack. I'd gone off the pill months previously. No need for it. When I told you it was safe, I meant to get a morning-after pill the next day.' She sighed, doubtful he could understand how she'd thought and felt afterwards.

'But you didn't,' he quietly prompted.

'No. You were gone without a word to me. Call it madness if you like, but I couldn't bring myself to do it.' She managed an ironic little smile. 'If a new life had been conceived by us, I felt it was meant to be. And I guess if I miscarry now, that's meant to be, too.'

Tears welled up. She quickly rolled her head across the pillow, turning her face away from him, swallowing hard to hold in the wave of grief. He would probably be relieved if she lost the baby, relieved to have no permanent tie on his plate. It was only she who wanted the child, loved knowing it was growing inside her, cherished the life she and Zack had made together.

'Please go...please...' she choked out, fiercely telling herself not to weep. It would knot up her muscles and she had to stay relaxed, think of the baby. She'd answered the critical questions, freed him of all responsibility.

She heard the scrape of his chair and the squeeze on her heart grew even tighter. He was leaving. A sense of utter desolation swept through her. A fool's dream...to think he might love her.

Then she felt warm fingers stroking down the hand lying closest to where he'd been sitting, strong fingers spreading hers apart, interlacing, gripping. 'I left you in the past, Catherine. I won't leave you alone tonight,' he said gruffly. 'You just rest now. I'll watch over you. Make sure nothing more goes wrong that I can help.'

She shut her eyes tight, but the tears spilled through her lashes and trickled down her cheeks. If he was angry with her, he wasn't showing it. Caring flowed from the heat of the hand holding hers and she was too weak to reject it. Caring might not be love but somehow it eased the emptiness that dragged at her, the fear of what she might be told tomorrow.

He stroked her hair with his other hand—gentle, soothing caresses. *Rest now,* he'd said, and his uncritical acceptance of her situation helped. Even his silent company helped. She felt no judgment in it, or her mind was too stressed out to sense any judgment. It was simply good to be assured she was not alone in a strange hospital, in a foreign country. Zack was here, looking after her.

She was fast asleep. The hand Zack still held had slackened into limp passivity some time ago. He'd been reluctant to let it go in case she stirred again and panicked at the sense of being on her own. Catherine was in L.A.—a huge distance away from her family and friends—because he'd called her. She hadn't contacted him about her pregnancy. It was his call that had brought her here. He felt his responsibility for taking care of her very keenly.

Her breathing was slow and even. Assured she was unlikely to awake for a while, Zack slowly slid his hand from hers and stood up, needing to stretch his stiff muscles, walk around the room a bit. A nurse had dropped by to check on Catherine and switched on a night-light when she saw the patient was settled. Everything was dimly visible. He could walk without bumping into furniture, and keep an eye on Catherine for any slight disturbance.

His mind was hopelessly clogged with the idea of her carrying his child—a tiny life inside her, which was under threat of ending before it had the chance to grow into what it could be. A son. A daughter. *His* son or daughter. He was stunned at how possessive he was coming to feel about it now that the initial shock had worn off.

Shades of his father?

Wanting himself immortalised by having a child with his genes step into his shoes?

Zack fiercely rejected the reflection. He would never be like his father in that respect. It was wrong. But what he'd done to Catherine was wrong, too...taking all she'd give then leaving her *without a word*. That stark little statement had really stung him. It hadn't been an accusation, just the simple truth.

Like everything else she said.

Simple truths.

She was too direct and honest to try to trap him.

And the one lie she had told—the *safe* lie—the truth was he hadn't wanted that night stopped any more than she did. If she'd told him she had no contraception, would he have left her to buy a packet of condoms? He shook his head, not sure of the answer, recalling how he had pressed her to absolve him of such a necessity.

So he could walk away afterwards without any concern.

Oh, he'd done a truly excellent job of that.

Not a word to her...until two months later when he'd wanted her again.

He suspected his call had thrown her into one hell of a dilemma—whether to tell him or not. He hadn't given her much chance to do so over the telephone. And he certainly hadn't been encouraging down at Santa Monica. But for the threatened miscarriage...would she have told him at all?

Had she told anyone?

He stood at her bedside, scrutinising the face that looked so peaceful and innocent in sleep, hiding her secrets. What did he really know of her? Only that she got to him as no other woman ever had. Was that enough to commit himself to a lifetime partnership?

If this pregnancy ended in a miscarriage...did he want to let Catherine go?

Should the baby be saved...? A primitive possessiveness surged over any reasonable train of thought. No way was he going to walk out of the life of his child. He had to secure his rights as a father. If that meant marriage...well, he wasn't averse to the idea of having Catherine as his wife. At least the sex was great, though sex wasn't everything in a marriage. Adjustments would have to be made. Whatever arrangement they came to, he *would* take care of her...take care of both her and their child, make sure they wanted for nothing.

His course was clear, provided there was no miscarriage.

If the baby was lost...

His mind instinctively shied from even considering that outcome. Tomorrow, after the scan...he would think about it then...if he had to.

CHAPTER TWELVE

'THERE is no heartbeat.'

No heartbeat...

Catherine felt her own heart stop. She closed her eyes. The doctor's words kept on ringing in her mind—a death knell for her baby.

'Are you sure?' Zack demanded harshly. 'Can you check again?'

'I have been trying to find it for some time, Mr. Freeman. There's nothing. I'm sorry, but there's no point in holding out any hope. Given the amount of bleeding, it was highly unlikely that...'

'All right!' Zack snapped.

Silence. Catherine floated in a sea of nothingness. No hope. No baby to love. Her heart had started beating again, sluggishly reluctant to bother with this life. She wanted to die, too.

'Miss Trent...'

The sympathetic tone in the doctor's voice forced her to open her eyelids and acknowledge him. Not his fault that her baby was dead. Fate had decided she couldn't have it after all.

'It's best you have a curette now.'

'Yes,' she agreed. Time to turn over another page. She wasn't pregnant with a new life anymore.

Zack came off his chair, clearly hating this outcome, wanting to fight it, helplessly conflicted because he couldn't. 'Was it the flight?' he demanded. 'I called Catherine to come here. It's a long flight from Sydney to L.A. The cabin pressure…'

'No. It should not cause a miscarriage,' the doctor assured him.

Zack looked wildly distraught. 'We had sex. Just hours before the bleeding started.'

The doctor sighed. 'Pregnancy does not preclude sex, Mr. Freeman. If everything was normal…'

'What do you mean…*normal?*'

It occurred to Catherine that Zack felt he had caused this and was racked with guilt over it. Through the haze of her own deep inner grief, she wondered why he cared so much. Had he decided he *wanted* their child? He'd stayed with her all night, all morning. She hadn't asked why, needing the comfort of some familiar presence and he'd provided it, but if he'd been silently making a claim on their child…

Gone now.

Beyond claiming.

No claim on Zack, either.

All gone.

'I mean a miscarriage occurs when something is wrong,' the doctor explained. 'That's not to say Miss Trent won't carry a pregnancy to full term another time around, just that this one wasn't right. Nature has its own way of correcting its mistakes.'

A mistake…

She shouldn't have let it happen, shouldn't have pinned so much on it…planning a life around a child she loved, a child she'd stolen from Zack without his knowledge. That was wrong from the start. Not like Livvy and Pete. They had done it right.

Zack kept on talking, expending a crackling energy that felt wrong, too. Futile. Out of place. It was finished, nothing left to argue over.

'Please…' It was an anguished croak. She looked hard at the doctor, appealing for finality. '…let's get on with it. Do what has to be done.'

Zack didn't know what to do. He couldn't help Catherine through this last grim procedure. It was out of his hands. The medical staff had wheeled her away. But he couldn't bring himself to leave the hospital.

It was Friday. He should be contacting people or letting them contact him. He took out his mobile phone. He'd switched the power off last night. His finger hovered over the button.

No.

Impossible to even think of business when Catherine…no life in her eyes…as dead as the child that might have been.

She'd wanted it.

And God help him, so had he.

Gut-wrenching disappointment that it wasn't to be.

He wandered around the hospital, had coffee in the canteen, found a place to shave and freshen up. They'd already brought Catherine back to her room when he returned to it. She was sleeping. Probably didn't want to wake up. Merciful oblivion. He could do with some of that himself. But he knew what had happened wasn't going to go away. It was a scar on his soul…the lost child.

Zack wasn't used to emotional turmoil. He made a plan and stuck to it, refining it as opportunities presented themselves, though always retaining his vision of where he wanted to go. The end goal.

Where Catherine Trent was concerned, his vision was very muddy. She kept knocking him off his straight-line thinking. The timing for a serious relationship was wrong, yet he had the sinking feeling that if he let her go now, he'd never get her back. And the wanting wasn't even sexual anymore.

He couldn't dismiss it on that basis. There was more to it. Difficult to define. Maybe it was the miscarriage messing him up, but it felt as though she was attached to some integral part of him and without her, there would be a very hollow place in his life that no one else would ever fill.

He picked up her hand, weighing it in his own— a light delicate hand, fine-boned slender fingers, neatly shaped nails. They weren't claws. He doubted she would have scratched him for child maintenance, let alone anything else. It was a soft, giving hand. She'd given him everything he'd wanted from her and made no demands on him. How many women were like that?

A memory from their first night together sprang into his mind—the blind date—Catherine saying she'd agreed to it to please her sister, him saying…

Then you have a giving nature. That's a trap in itself, Catherine.

Her answer— *Oh, the giving only goes so far.*

Him, curious— *What would you take, given the chance?*

That's a big question.

And you don't intend to answer it yet?

That would spoil the game.

He'd laughed, thinking it was a flirtatious game, but none of it had been a game to her. She'd given twice. Unreservedly. And then she'd taken what she'd wanted—the chance of having a child from their union. And now she was left with nothing. Unless he could supply her with something she considered worth having.

Her fingers fluttered, subconsciously protesting their imprisonment. She was waking up. His heart kicked, speeding up his pulse rate, shooting much-needed oxygen to his overworked brain. He had to establish some kind of positive rapport with Catherine. Whatever it was they had together…he didn't want it to end here.

A frown creased her brow. She moaned and turned on her side away from him, drawing her legs up to scrunch herself into a protective ball. She hadn't opened her eyes, wasn't aware of his presence, and Zack suddenly felt like a voyeur to deeply private grief. Yet it might also be physical pain.

'Catherine,' he called urgently. 'Should I get a nurse or doctor?'

Her head whipped around on the pillow. Startled eyes. Puzzlement. 'You're still here?'

'Are you okay?'

She sighed and carefully shifted her body to face

him. 'I'll cope with it, Zack. You don't have to stay and nursemaid me.'

'I brought you to L.A., Catherine.'

'I made the choice. I don't hold you to blame for anything. And you've been more than generous, fixing all this for me. I'm sorry…'

'Don't apologise. I'm the one who should be apologising.'

She looked bewildered. 'What for?'

'Because I…' He gestured an appeal for some stay of judgment as he struggled for words to explain his feelings. 'Because I did this to you,' he finally got out.

'No, Zack. I did this to myself,' she said with firm clarity, then grimaced. 'Though not the miscarriage.'

Her face started to crumple and she fought for composure. Zack stood up and paced around the room, wanting to take her in his arms and comfort her, yet sensing such a move would be unwelcome. Possibly hurtful. He wanted to reach out to her but he didn't know how to. Never in his whole life had he felt so…inadequate, mentally floundering, and deeply frustrated by his inability to resolve what should be done with Catherine.

'I want to go home, Zack.'

The flat statement pulled him up at the end of her bed. He stared at her—this woman who tugged so strongly on him. He didn't see her beauty, her desirability. He saw the distance yawning between them, the determination in her eyes to break away from him.

'I'm to stay here overnight,' she ran on matter-offactly. 'But after the doctor sees me in the morning...if there's no problem...I'll contact Qantas and...'

'No. It's too soon. You should give yourself more time to recover. I'll take you back to the hotel and look after you, Catherine. At least stay the full week,' he argued forcefully.

Her head rolled in a pained negative. 'You only wanted me with you for the sex, Zack.' Her eyes mocked anything else he might say. 'I can't deliver,' she said flatly. 'And my staying would only make us both miserable, continually reminding us...'

She swallowed hard and closed her eyes.

'I don't want to let you go like this,' he burst out.

'Please...' Her throat moved convulsively. '...it would be...a kindness.'

Kindness... Zack was completely torn by that word. It forced him to examine his behaviour towards her. Everything on his terms. Certainly he'd given her choices but there'd been no consideration for her feelings behind them. No kindness.

You were gone without a word to me.

He couldn't justify that. It was an indictment of how totally selfish he had been. All he'd ever thought about was what he wanted.

It was her right to have the last word now.

'Leave it to me,' he said with grim decisiveness. 'I'll call Qantas and line up a return flight for you. Ensure you'll get a seat.'

She visibly sagged with relief. 'Thank you.' Her gaze dropped from his. Her fingers plucked at the bedcover. 'I'm sorry about...I know the Academy Awards is a big night for you...'

'Don't worry about it. Right now I couldn't care less.' It was the truth.

'I didn't mean to...'

'Catherine, please...'

The anguish in his voice flicked her gaze back to his, a pained wondering in her eyes. 'You've been so good about all this, Zack. I promise I'll pay you back. The hospital costs and...'

'Stop!' He glared at her, fury boiling up at being so pointedly counted out of what should have been shared. 'It was my child, too. I would have paid anything to save it. At least grant me that right, Catherine.'

'I'm sorry.' Tears filmed her eyes. 'I didn't think...didn't know...'

'That I would care?' he cut in savagely.

She nodded, biting her lips.

The anger that had so quickly surged, drowned just as quickly in the swimming vulnerability of her eyes. How could he rail at her judgment of him? He'd given her no reason to believe he would care. He sucked in a deep breath in an attempt to calm himself.

'Responsibility for the medical expenses is all mine,' he growled. 'No argument. And I'll get you on a flight home as soon as it's feasible. Okay?'

'Thank you.' It was a husky little whisper. Her head was bent, lashes lowered, hiding her eyes.

There was no triumph for him in her submission to his will. She looked defeated. He felt defeated. It might be a kindness to let her go, but every muscle in his body ached to fight her decision. The whole room seemed to pulse with the tension of things unsaid on both sides. Which couldn't be good for her after all she'd been through.

'Well, now that's settled, I'll leave you to rest,' he said bruskly. 'Don't worry about anything. I'll let you know what I've organised when it's done. Okay?'

'Yes.' She raised eyes that looked deathly weary. 'I would have told you about our child in the end, Zack. Then it would have been your choice, whether you wanted to be a father or not. It's probably for the best…that you don't have to make that choice now. No ties…' Her attempt at a smile wobbled. 'That's good for you, isn't it?'

It was like a punch to the heart—all the more lethal because it was what he'd told himself countless times since he'd first met Catherine. Ties held you down. Ties prevented you from going after opportunities that closed too quickly if you weren't on the spot, all primed to take them up. Yet faced with that argument from her, he wanted to disown it. Vehemently.

'You can put all this behind you and move on,' she pressed. 'It's easier than…' She took a deep breath and released it in a shuddering sigh. 'You know what I mean. You can have my things sent here from the hotel. I'll get to the airport by myself. There's no need…'

'You *want* me to say goodbye now?'

Her gaze wavered from his. 'You probably should be meeting with other people...'

'Don't make my decisions for me, Catherine. If you'd prefer not to see me anymore, say so. Otherwise I'll be back to visit you tonight. And tomorrow. If you *must* go home, I intend to make sure you're fit enough to fly out before you do and I'll accompany you to the airport and see you into the care of the flight attendants.'

She stared at him, not understanding his motivation. Which was fair enough, because he didn't understand it himself. All he knew—and knew with absolute certainty—was he needed time to sort this inner turmoil through before any final line was drawn. Since she didn't rush to reject his plan, Zack pressed it as a confirmed fact.

'I'll be back,' he stated decisively and left the room before she could make some belated protest.

Catherine stared at the closed door. She had invited Zack to close it, expected him to close it, but he was coming back to open it again. Or so he said.

But why would he?

Her mind jammed with jumbled-up emotions.

They hurt.

Everything hurt.

She curled herself up under the bedcover, buried her face in the pillow and wept for all her lost dreams.

CHAPTER THIRTEEN

THEY sat in the first-class lounge at LAX, waiting for the Qantas flight to Sydney to be called. Catherine glanced at Zack who'd fallen silent, withdrawing into himself, a tense brooding look on his face. She had no idea what he was thinking, or what purpose had been served for him in keeping her company until she left for home. All she knew was the departure time was very close now and the past hour with him had stretched her nerves to breaking point.

It had only ever been sex for him and that was patently over. Ever since she'd made the decision to get out of his life as fast as possible, he'd made no reference to the intimacy they'd shared, gave no indication that he might want it resumed at a later date. No doubt he knew, as she did, it couldn't ever be the same as before. So why had he bothered with the courtesy of treating her like a valued visitor?

Last night and most of today he had been questioning her about her life and her job, whether she considered her work a career worth pursuing or simply the means to a good income, what she liked doing, what she disliked. It was as though he was finally assessing her as a fully rounded person, not just seeing her as a sexually desirable woman—a strange bittersweet experience for Catherine, coming too late

152

to mean he might want a serious relationship with her.

Most likely their conversations had been about keeping her mind—and his—off the pregnancy that had been so traumatically terminated. She had to concede they had helped in that regard, more so when he talked about his work and the kind of things he planned to try in the future—animated films he wanted his own company to produce. That had given her a glimpse of the visions he nursed, what drove him to keep moving on.

Zack Freeman was never going to stand still. It was amazing that he'd actually taken these few days out to be with her, holding her hand through the worst of it. Maybe he had felt some obligation towards her, dragged into it because she'd revealed so much of her own feelings in getting pregnant to him. Guilt...kindness...giving her time he hadn't given before. He was probably champing at the bit now, thinking of what he'd do the moment she was gone.

'Boarding call for Qantas flight QF12 to Sydney, Australia. Will passengers please proceed to gate one-two-two?'

Catherine picked up her bag and rose quickly from the armchair, relieved that the strain of this last togetherness with Zack was over. He was slower to react to the announcement, unfolding himself from his chair rather than springing up. It focused her attention on his height and the powerful physique that made him so *male,* and everything inside her quivered at this last farewell.

This was the man she had chosen to father her child.

This was the man she had recklessly loved.

Forcing herself to face the inevitable end, she thrust out a hand and lifted her gaze to his. 'Goodbye…'

'No!'

The word exploded from him. Her hand was caught in both of his, the doubly possessive grip preventing her from pulling it free. His dark eyes probed hers with searing intensity, making her heart skitter even more painfully at this sudden impasse.

'I don't want you to leave, Catherine.'

Sheer anguish voiced her reply. 'Zack, it won't work…'

'I don't mean the week I'd planned to spend with you,' he rapped out dismissively. 'This is something else.'

'I have to go,' she cried in panic, not believing that anything he suggested could be anything but painful in these circumstances. 'The flight has been called.'

'We could fly to Las Vegas. Get married.'

She stared incredulously at the blazing conviction in his eyes. 'Get…*married?*' Had she heard right?

'Yes. There's nothing to stop us, is there? It won't be the end of the world if you resigned from your job, stayed with me.'

Her job meant nothing.

Staying with him meant everything.

Yet to ask her to marry him now…

All those questions yesterday and today…had he

been considering this proposal all along? Seeing if she would fit the role of his wife? Catherine was utterly dumbfounded by this move. No way had she seen it coming. It was too big a leap from the free-wheeling position he'd stated just two days ago.

'Catherine, we can have other children,' he pressed, as though that was the ultimate persuasion.

She instantly recoiled from it—mentally, emotionally and physically—her stomach cramping over the empty space that had been left by the miscarriage. This wasn't right. His mind was somehow stuck on their lost child. This proposal could be nothing more than an aberrational moment that would be regretted within hours or days.

'No...' She had to choke the word out. Her throat had tightened up. Her chest, too. She shook her head vehemently to get the message across.

'You wanted a baby,' he argued. 'You wanted me to be the father. So let's do it properly. Get married. Set up a home...'

'Stop! Please...stop!' Her mind was spinning. He was offering the biggest temptation of all. Her heart was thumping a wild yes to it, not caring why it was being offered, responding instinctively to the things she'd yearned to hear—married to Zack Freeman, having a family...

He frowned at her resistance. 'I swear I'll look after you. I always live up to my commitments, Catherine.'

Yes, he did, but *commitments* sounded so cold. Where was the passion for her, the love she craved?

'Once I give my word...' he went on.

Like a contract, not the love of a lifetime. He wasn't talking of love. Her need to hear more from him burst into speech.

'Your word is not enough,' she cried, desperate to reach into the heart of the man.

'Why not?' he challenged fiercely. 'What more do you want?'

'I want...' Was she mad to push for more? But how could she bear to be his wife if she was just one of many women he found desirable? It made her too vulnerable. If she plunged into this marriage and then found...no...no.... Words spilled out, begging for the right response from him. 'I want the man I marry to love me.'

'Love...' He shook his head as though it was some irrelevant concept, a vexatious sidetrack to be quickly bypassed. Only the end goal mattered and he had that in his sights. 'Of course you're very special to me,' he declared impatiently. 'Do you think I'd ask *any* woman to marry me?'

'How special, Zack?' she challenged, needing to nail it down. 'So special you don't want to spend your life without me? No other woman will do?'

'Yes. That's it. That's precisely it.'

It sounded too glib, like he was quickly feeding back what she wanted to hear, no pause to express something more deeply personal to him in his own words. And she remembered the sting of neglect, the flame of jealousy. Accusing words tumbled out of the torment of loving a man who could not possibly love her.

'Then how come you had another woman on your

arm at the Golden Globes night, very soon after you'd been with me three months ago? And a different woman again at the BAFTA Awards night, just before you called me to join you for the Academy Awards. I saw shots of you on news programs…'

'Those women were simply…handy,' he said with a grimace, disliking being put on that highly ambivalent spot.

It didn't soothe the hurt of all the silence from him, the hurt that he found other women attractive enough to share important occasions in his life with *them,* not *her.*

And only two days ago had come the warning that this third occasion together was only another one-off—a longer time but to be ended in the same way, no promise of more. It didn't add up to love in Catherine's mind. It didn't even add up to extra special.

The only difference was he knew she'd fallen pregnant to him and she'd lost the child that might have been. His child. Their child. Obviously the whole thing had become very personal to him, linking this proposal to having other children, but it was the wrong time, the wrong place, the wrong sentiment.

It didn't fill her soul with joy.

She needed her love to be returned, not used.

Her baby would have loved her back.

But Zack…the hand of harsh reality squeezed her heart, forcing out the temptation it had nursed. She couldn't accept his proposal. Being married to him would be a hell of uncertainty and fear. That was the truth of it and as much as she might want to overlook it, how could she?

She looked at him with all the emptiness she felt and laid her position on the line. 'I don't want to be a *handy* wife, Zack. I need my husband to think of me as irreplaceable. The *one* woman he wants above all others. I don't believe you can honestly say that, so please…let me go now.'

'Catherine…' His hands gripped more tightly.

'No.' It took every scrap of her will to fight the blazing determination in his eyes. 'You'll think better of this tomorrow. Or the next day. Or the next.' She gave him a savagely ironic smile. 'This, too, will pass.'

A battle light gleamed. 'And if it doesn't?'

That was his problem.

She was sure he'd find some *handy* solution to it.

'I'm going home,' she threw at him, unable to take any more argument with her heart and soul aching so badly. She wrenched her hand from his and held it up to ward off any further attempt to delay her. 'Goodbye, Zack. Thank you for seeing me off.'

She left him without a backward glance, desperately certain in her own mind she was right to go. She was through with making rash decisions where Zack Freeman was concerned. If he'd truly cared for her, he would have shown it by considering *her* feelings, asking her what *she* wanted.

A quickie marriage in Las Vegas.

On his terms.

Where was there any love for her in that?

No family wedding like Livvy's and Pete's.

A shoddy affair, telling her she wasn't worth much time to him. Just a convenience. And a baby machine. She didn't care that he could well afford to look after his wife and family. Not all the money in the world could buy her into that situation.

So she told herself in a rage of pain and pride as she made herself march towards the designated departure gate. Yet every step of the way, her body was begging for Zack to follow her, stop her, convince her she was wrong, heal the hurts and make everything better so she could believe a marriage between them could and would work.

But he didn't come after her.

Didn't stop her.

She joined the line of passengers boarding the aeroplane. She was so tense and tremulous she dropped her ticket when it was her turn to put it through the processing machine. Every second was an agony of waiting for a shout or a hand to clamp on her shoulder.

But nothing stopped her from entering the boarding tunnel. No call came for her to disembark before the flight took off. Once the big Qantas jet started rolling down the tarmac, Catherine sagged into a huge black hole of hopelessness.

It was over.

The baby...

The chance of marrying Zack Freeman...

She'd lost both of them...

Forever.

CHAPTER FOURTEEN

FOR the full week she was supposed to be away, Catherine left her answering machine on, not wanting to speak to anyone. She listened to the messages. Nothing from Zack. Which was only to be expected. It was stupid to feel tense every time the telephone rang. Clearly he had accepted her rejection and was probably grateful for it before she'd even left Los Angeles.

Mostly the calls were from Livvy, increasingly impatient with her sister's absence.

'Where are you?' she demanded on one message.

On her last call came an exasperated, 'Okay, Mum tells me you've gone off on a week's vacation. You could have told me, too. So call me as soon as you're back.'

Livvy...whom she was sure was still happily pregnant. Catherine didn't want to hear baby news. The grief over her own loss could be too easily tapped. But she couldn't block her sister out of her life because Livvy had what she would never have now. That was too mean and miserable. Within a reasonable response time, Catherine steeled herself to chat as normally as she could to her very voluble sister.

'At last!' Livvy greeted with emphatic satisfaction. 'Where have you been?'

'Oh, just up to the Blue Mountains, communing

with nature,' she answered. It wasn't a complete lie. She had driven up there yesterday to get herself out of the apartment and memories that crowded in on her at home. 'Is everything okay with you? Why all the calls?'

'Everything's fine. Wonderful! Did you watch the Academy Awards on TV?' Livvy pressed eagerly.

Catherine's heart turned over. This had to be about Zack. 'No,' she said flatly. The flight home crossed the dateline, losing a day. If Zack had won an award he would have been presented with it while she was still flying over the ocean. Not that she would have watched the ceremony anyway. Why torture herself with might-have-beens?

'Zack won for achievement in visual effects,' Livvy announced as though it was a triumph that she and Pete were still celebrating.

'Well, good for him!' Catherine responded, trying to inject some enthusiasm into her voice.

'And you'll never know what...' Livvy ran on excitedly.

'What?' Catherine obliged.

'He mentioned me and Pete in his acceptance speech.'

'Well, that must have been a nice surprise.' It surprised her, too.

'*And* the fact we're having a baby.'

Catherine's stomach contracted.

'I don't know how he knew. Pete hadn't told him. He must have got the news from his mother who's very friendly with Pete's mother.'

I told him.

'Anyhow, there he was, up on stage receiving an Oscar, and Pete and I were expecting him to rave on about the movie and thank all the people who'd helped to bring his vision to life, which he did, very briefly. Then he said...I know the words off by heart because we videoed it...so listen to this, Catherine.'

'I'm listening,' she said, her nerves in a total mess again.

'I quote... "I guess it could be said this is a pinnacle of achievement for me. Creative achievement. But the far greater creation is a beautiful new life. I've just heard that my oldest friend in Australia, Pete Raynor, and his lovely wife, Livvy, are expecting a baby. Their first child. I think that's worth more than a thousand Oscars. Congratulations, Pete."'

Their first child...

Had her miscarriage still been preying on his mind, above and beyond the crowning recognition of his work? Was he finding it much more difficult to set aside than it had been to set *her* aside? Her heart ached unbearably as Livvy rattled on.

'Wasn't that great? Pete was so thrilled. I couldn't believe it, being named like that on an internationally televised show. And the applause was terrific. The camera followed Zack back to his seat in the auditorium. Pete was saying it would give the woman he was with ideas, but the odd thing was, he didn't have anyone with him. The seat beside him was empty.'

Her seat.

Had she been...*irreplaceable?*

An overwhelming sadness clogged her mind. It was like pulling words out through quicksand to make adequate replies to Livvy's happy carry-on. Eventually she managed to end the call, desperately fending off an invitation to view the video, saying she was heavily booked up with activities for the next few weeks. In fact, she was running late for an appointment now.

It was a lie.

She hated telling lies.

But it had been the only defence she could come up with. The hurt was too raw to share with anyone, especially if... Had she been wrong to reject Zack's proposal? Had she misunderstood his motives, misinterpreted his words and actions? Maybe he would have been faithful to their marriage, cleaving only to her...

Stop it, stop it, stop it! she savagely berated herself.

It was done.

Finished.

Too late to take back.

So he was deeply affected by the loss of their child. It didn't mean he loved her. The empty seat was just an empty seat. It couldn't be concluded that he couldn't bear to be with anyone else. There was no point in tormenting herself with such thoughts. If he'd loved her, everything would have been different.

Catherine kept telling herself this, day after day, week after week. She worked hard at her job, avoided meeting Livvy in person, held endless one-sided conversations with her goldfish who listened sympathetically to her emotional outpourings and her best attempts at logical reasoning. In this regard, Rhett and Scarlet were her perfect companions.

She told herself she was managing okay…until the parcel came. It was a box—a box sent from London—and the sender's name was Zack Freeman.

Zack felt uncharacteristically tense as he belted himself into his seat for take off on the long flight from London to Sydney. He'd failed with Catherine last time—had deserved to fail—and it was impossible to forecast her response to his message. Had enough time gone by? Had he waited too long?

He vividly recalled the bitter irony of her words… *This, too, will pass.* But it hadn't. And it never would. He'd been trying to block Catherine Trent out of his mind for over a year. It had proved impossible. And now…now he couldn't block her out of his heart. Nor did he want to. She was his woman. Somehow he had to undo the damage he'd done so she would accept him back into her life.

Had the rose started that process for him?

It had been a risky gamble, posting it to her. She'd remember him taking it out of her hair the night of Pete's wedding—a prelude to the intimacy they'd shared, after which he'd left her *without a word.* Would it mean anything to her that he'd taken the rose with him? She might think it had represented a crass souvenir of a great night of sex. He couldn't blame her if she did. Yet it wasn't true.

He'd kept the rose because instinctively he'd wanted to keep her. At the time he wouldn't let himself go down that track. Not until he knew about the baby—how much it had meant to her—how much it had suddenly meant to him. Their child. His and Catherine's. It had gradually seeped into his soul—the rightness of their being together. He'd been so blindly stubborn not to recognise it before.

Bad move—his proposal of marriage at LAX. Too quick. Totally inappropriate after the miscarriage. And lacking in credibility in the light of all he'd done and not done.

Her walking away from him had been one hell of a wake-up call, underlining how she had read his behaviour—every action totally self-centred, not even pausing to consider where she had been coming from, nor asking where she wanted to go. It had to be different this time. Very different. He was extremely conscious of the thin line he'd be treading. Any mistake…

The airline steward offered a tray of drinks. He took a glass of orange juice. No champagne for him. Champagne was for celebrating and he had nothing to celebrate on this trip.

'Are we running late?' he asked, impatient to get on his way to Catherine.

'No, sir. We'll be taking off on schedule in ten minutes,' came the confident assurance.

Ten minutes…plus over twenty hours in the air…more time waiting through the stopover in Singapore…it was a long haul to Sydney…and he wasn't even sure Catherine would meet him. Had the note he'd put in the box with the rose said enough to win him another chance with her?

Once again he weighed the words he'd written—

words he'd formulated and reformulated dozens of times during the weeks he'd already waited....

Catherine—

It's long past the next day and the next and the next. No amount of time will wear away the connection I feel with you. Can we meet again?

I'll be in Sydney on the first day of May. There's a rose garden in the botanical gardens, just down from the Macquarie Street entrance. From twelve noon I'll be there waiting for you.

Zack.

If she didn't come...every primitive male instinct pushed to go to her apartment and break down the door if necessary, smash any barrier she put up, take her in his arms, make wild passionate love to her, force her to respond.

But would such action work?

In the end, the choice was hers.

What did Catherine want? That was the critical question. This meeting had to be based on giving, not taking—persuasion, not force.

The steward came and collected his glass.

The jumbo jet started rolling down the runway.

The die was cast.

CHAPTER FIFTEEN

THE first day of May...

Catherine stood on the corner of Macquarie Street where the big iron gates to the botanical gardens were wide open, inviting the public to wander in and enjoy the ambience of beautiful trees and flowers. She doubted such pleasantries would even impinge on her consciousness if she entered these grounds.

It was past noon. A steely pride had overriden her usual passion for punctuality. No way would she be found waiting for Zack Freeman. She'd allowed an extra half hour in case he'd run into unavoidable delays, but if his word meant anything, he should be in the rose garden by now.

Still the question hovered in her mind—to meet him or not? It would open everything up again. To what end? More pain? He was in Sydney today. Where tomorrow? Was this meeting with her being fitted into a business trip? What if he just wanted small bites of her life, reconnecting at his convenience? She'd die if that were the case, die of humiliation that she'd turned up to his call.

Yet...the rose he'd kept and sent to her...meeting in a public rose garden in the middle of the day...surely it had to mean more than just sex on his mind. If she didn't go and find out, the torment of wondering what she might have missed would haunt her for the rest of her life.

Her legs felt like jelly. It was a fine sunny day but it didn't warm the chill in her heart. She forced her feet forward, determined now on her course. Signs directed her to the path she had to follow. It wouldn't take long, she told herself, to know the outcome of this meeting.

The sheer physical impact of seeing Zack again caught her completely unprepared. Emotional turmoil had clouded her memory of how it was with him. Her feet came to a dead halt as she took in the shock of his effect on her; the instant quickening of her pulse, the magnetic pull on every muscle of her body, the frightening awareness of her sexuality and her vulnerability to the power of his.

And he wasn't even looking at her!

He was seated on a bench seat under a tree at the other end of the rose garden. His body was hunched forward, head bent, elbows resting on his knees, hands linked, obviously deep in thought. Despite this tightly contained pose, he radiated an intense energy which she knew would engulf her the moment he was alerted to her presence.

A sense of panic jangled her nerves. It was dangerous, letting Zack get close again. She couldn't trust herself not to respond to him. Before she could decide what to do about it, his head jerked up and his dark riveting gaze held her locked into his personal force-field. No retreat possible.

He stood in one swift fluid action, then seemed to come towards her in slow motion, dominating her vision, dominating her mind, dominating her heart. She had no control over any of them, and in her stomach grew the sickening sense that nothing was ever going to change how she felt with Zack Freeman. She was too deeply connected to him.

'What do you want with me?' she blurted out, fighting for a defensive foothold that would guard her against falling into some disastrous decision.

The direct challenge halted him an arm's length away, not far enough for her to feel safe, but at least giving her some space. His eyes scoured hers, undoubtedly looking for chinks of weakness. She stood her ground and stared back unflinchingly, resolved on getting answers before he touched her.

'What do you want with me, Catherine?' he returned quietly, skewering her with her own question.

'You speak first,' she demanded, refusing to take that bait. It would leave her with no pride at all. 'It was you who asked for this meeting, Zack. Not me.'

He nodded. A wisp of a smile curved his lips and his eyes softened with a caressing warmth. 'I'm glad you came.'

'I can go just as easily,' she flashed back, feeling herself start to melt inside and stiffening her spine to counter any crumbling.

'I know.' He gestured to the bench seat. 'Would you like to sit or stroll? A family group is coming down the path and we're blocking it here.'

'I'll sit for a while,' she decided, glad there were other people around. Being alone with Zack was not a good idea.

He turned aside to let her fall into step with him

and made no attempt to take her hand or arm as they walked along to the bench seat he'd vacated. He was dressed in black casual clothes: jeans, T-shirt, leather jacket. Probably travelling clothes. She had defiantly dressed in yellow. At least her sweater was yellow. Her skirt was mostly black with a zigzag pattern of white and yellow. She had wanted to look bright, on top of her world without him.

It was a lie. Amazing how good she was getting at lies when it came to her involvement with Zack Freeman. Desperate, protective lies.

'Have you just arrived in Sydney?' she asked, probing for his current circumstances.

'Yesterday.'

'Is this a business trip?'

'You're my only business here, Catherine.'

'You've come from London just to see me?'

'Yes.'

'No other purpose? No wedding, no award, no deal waiting in the wings that you have to hurry off to?' she tossed out flippantly.

'Not this time,' he answered grimly.

A fierce satisfaction flared through Catherine. At least she wasn't a secondary item on this visit to Australia. There was no other agenda. He'd come for her. Yet that begged the question, 'What if I hadn't turned up, Zack?' She sneaked a quick look at him, wary of taking too much for granted.

He caught her glance and flashed a wry little smile. 'I was considering that situation when you arrived. Should I respect your wishes or should I storm the barricades? I'm relieved not to have to make that decision.'

Storm the barricades... Her heart fluttered at the passion inherent in those words. Could she resist him? Did she want to? They reached the seat and she was careful to keep some distance between them as they sat. There were many questions to be answered and the desire he stirred in her could well be flattened by his replies.

'Okay, here I am. Tell me what this is about for you,' she invited, deliberately evading eye contact with him, fixing her gaze on the nearest rose bed. She could feel his tension vibrating around her, a harnessed aggression that burned under the surface of his control. It increased her own tension and she clung to a calm facade, determinedly hiding her inner turbulence.

She was aware of him leaning forward, resting his elbows on his knees again. 'I'll start at the beginning. Our blind date. I wasn't expecting to meet a woman who'd get under my skin.' His deep voice carried a liberal dash of irony.

'A one-night wonder for you,' she muttered mockingly.

It made him pause, reflect. 'I guess I've given you no reason to think it was any more,' he said ruefully.

'You want me to believe it was?' She shot him a derisive look. 'No contact with me for nine months. And then I was only an incidental on the night of Pete's and Livvy's wedding. You hadn't come for me. You barely acknowledged my presence until you decided you wanted sex with me again.'

He grimaced and shook his head. 'It wasn't like that. I realise it must look that way to you, but it wasn't like that.'

'No?'

'No!' It was a vehement denial, his eyes burning through her scorn, projecting intense conviction.

She wrenched her gaze from his and returned it to the rose garden, frightened of letting his magnetic energy sweep away all reason. 'Then how was it, Zack?' she demanded coldly, not letting the heat from him influence her.

He sucked in a deep breath. She didn't care if she was putting him through some mental wringer. Her need to know the truth of his feelings for her was paramount.

'When I first met you I had a three-year plan,' he stated, obviously deciding to give her the big picture. 'All work,' he said significantly. 'I didn't want to put the effort into building and maintaining a relationship with any woman. It was easy enough to pick up a companion for a social function if needed.'

'With a night of sex thrown in for good measure.' The bitter little comment spilled out. She gritted her teeth against saying any more, hating the fact that he'd put her in the same category as other casual sex partners.

'You were different, Catherine,' he quickly asserted.

Inwardly she bristled. He certainly hadn't treated her any differently to the others who had passed through his life.

'What we shared that night on the beach...I tried

to dismiss it as a sexual fantasy but you remained too real in my mind. I resented the continual intrusion of the memory, tried to downplay it, reason it away, took other women to bed to blot it out. I won't deny that. Won't lie about it, either. Though I did it less and less because it was *you* I wanted and every other woman was a frustration because she wasn't you.'

Was that supposed to be a compliment? It was certainly a backhander if it was—the unforgettable woman he'd do anything to forget. He made her sound like a curse—a blight on his life.

'It messed me up to such an extent I decided not to go to Pete's wedding because *you* would be there, and I didn't want what I thought of as my obsession with you aggravated.'

'Obsession?' It shocked her into looking at him again.

He raised his hands in a kind of exasperated appeal. 'What would you call it? There I was, not even prepared to be Pete's best man because you were sure to be Livvy's chief bridesmaid and if I had to partner you all throughout the wedding…it would get me in deeper with you and mess me around even more.'

'But you did come…' *And avoided me like the plague for most of the wedding.*

'I was angry with myself for letting Pete down. My oldest friend. And I was angry at investing you with so much power over my life. In the end, I had to come, not only for Pete, but to prove to myself that what I felt about you was more fantasy than reality. I wanted you to be...' He hesitated, grimacing over the truth before admitting it. '...something I could finally dismiss.'

It did make sense, Catherine slowly conceded, fitting his thoughts to how he had acted at the wedding.

'But I found myself wanting you so badly...I couldn't stand watching that guy dance with you, touching you...'

The aggression—fiercely possessive aggression. Yes, it did make sense. She frowned, dropping her gaze from his, wondering how much more she hadn't understood...from his viewpoint.

'I had to have you again.'

The throb of passion in his voice echoed through her own heart. She'd felt the same way, despite the lack of any communication from him. The compulsion to take what she could have of Zack Freeman had been overwhelming, even to letting herself get pregnant so she could have his child.

'And still I resented the power you had to do this to me, Catherine. I tried to exercise control over it. Then control didn't seem to matter. Only you mattered. I didn't want to wake you when I had to leave because if I did...' He sighed. 'It was easier to go while you were asleep. I took the rose. I wanted to keep something of you.'

Like she'd wanted to keep part of him.

'I had work commitments and I couldn't see a place for you in the schedule I had planned. But it was worse this time. I couldn't keep you out of my mind. You haunted my nights.'

Days and nights for me, she recalled, especially after learning a baby had been conceived.

'Catherine…look at me!' he commanded.

Her head snapped up. The angst in his eyes begged her belief.

'The women I took to the award ceremonies…they were just window-dressing. I didn't have sex with them. Didn't want to. In fact, it was after barely tolerating the model I was with at the BAFTA Awards that I called you to meet me in L.A. *You* were the one I wanted to be with.'

A wave of sadness rolled through her at the memory of her miscarriage in Los Angeles. It had thrown a black cloud over everything. Though before she'd told him she was pregnant… 'You still didn't see a place in your life for me, Zack. It was just for a week.'

'That was the plan,' he conceded heavily. 'I don't know that it would have stuck, given a whole week together.'

He fell silent.

Catherine knew instinctively he was remembering—mourning—their lost child. As she did.

He heaved another deep sigh. 'I'm sorry I…'

'You did everything you could,' she rushed out, not wanting the grief of that time recalled. When she'd needed his help, he'd given it unstintingly. That was the important thing to remember. And what Zack had been telling her rang true. But what it would mean for her in the future, she still didn't know.

'I was wrong not to make a place for you,

Catherine,' he said gruffly. 'I don't know if you can forgive all I haven't done where you are concerned, but I swear I'll do my best to make it up to you, if you'll give me the chance.'

She understood the vision he had for his work. It was a big part of him. He'd never rest, never feel satisfied, until it had all come alive. The conflict she'd represented in Zack's mind had been real and enduring. There was no longer any basis for the bitterness she'd nursed. It ebbed away.

'Where would I fit, Zack?' she asked, looking at him now with very clear eyes. The murk of the past had been dissipated by his honesty, but the same honesty showed her that any path ahead for them was crowded with other factors that could take their toll on any relationship.

His mouth quirked into an appealing little smile. 'I thought we could create our own fishbowl.'

She shook her head, not comprehending what he meant.

'There'd be a very busy world going on outside it, Catherine, but it needn't touch what we have together. If you're willing to be Scarlet to my Rhett, we could swim around, side by side...'

'All the time?' she asked incredulously, not having dared to hope for so much.

'That's what I'd like.' He searched her eyes for any objections. 'But you must tell me what you want. I'll try to accommodate...'

Her hand lifted, pressing soft, silencing fingers to his mouth. 'I want to be with you wherever you go,' she said, letting him see the truth of her heart shining in her eyes.

He covered her hand with his, pressed a long, lingering kiss of warm promise on her palm. Catherine's heart turned over. Before she dared think it, he said, 'I love you Catherine Trent.' Then… 'Will you be my wife?'

'Yes,' she whispered.

His smile was dazzling—relief, joy, intense pleasure in her. Still holding her left hand, he reached into the pocket of his jacket and drew out a small jeweller's box. Catherine stared in utter amazement as he flicked it open to reveal a huge diamond solitaire ring.

'Diamonds are forever,' he said with relish, and slid it onto the third finger of her left hand.

'We're going to do this right,' he stated, determined purpose pouring from him as he swept on. 'We'll visit your family tonight, announce our engagement, plan a wedding…'

'A wedding?' Catherine repeated dazedly.

'You'd like Livvy to stand by you and I'll ask Pete to be my best man. Tomorrow we'll visit my mother. She'll want to be in the thick of things, too. In fact…'

'Zack…'

'Have I said something wrong?' he asked anxiously.

'No…' She laughed, bubbling over with so many happy emotions she couldn't begin to express them. 'You really were going to storm the barricades,' she finally spluttered out.

He grinned. 'I certainly didn't plan to leave without you this time, Catherine.'

She sobered, remembering the last time he'd proposed marriage. 'I'm thirty-two, Zack. If we're going to have…other children…'

The twinkle left his eyes, too. He gently stroked her cheek. 'No waiting. And when you do fall pregnant again I'll be right beside you all the way, looking after you as best I can.'

Neither of them would forget the one they'd lost, yet perhaps its brief innocent life had bonded them more deeply together.

'I can promise you I won't make the same mistakes with our children that my father made with me,' Zack said with considerable feeling, then made a wry little grimace. 'But I'll probably make others. It'll be your job to correct me, Catherine. And I'll listen. If Dad had ever listened to my mother…' He shook his head. 'My mother's a great person. You'll like her.'

'I hope she likes me.'

'I know she will. You're both great people.'

Zack rose from the bench seat, drawing Catherine to her feet and wrapping her in a tender embrace. 'Let's make this a new start,' he murmured.

'Yes,' she agreed, her heart swelling with the same need to get it right this time. 'I love you, too, Zack. That's a good place to start.'

They kissed.

And the connection between them went soul-deep.

There…in a garden full of roses.

CHAPTER SIXTEEN

SEPTEMBER... The first month of Spring in Australia...and the day was bright and sunny, perfect for the wedding.

'The flowers have arrived!' Livvy yelled from downstairs. 'I'm bringing ours up.'

Catherine stepped into the dress she'd chosen to wear and pulled it up, carefully sliding her arms through the armholes. She was positioning the bodice properly on her shoulders as Livvy sailed into the bedroom. 'I need help with the back fastening,' she appealed to her sister.

'Oh, wow!' Livvy breathed at first sight of *the dress* on Catherine. She quickly laid the flowers on the bed and moved to complete the fitting. When it was done, they both stared at the reflection in the mirror. 'That is fabulous!' Livvy declared in absolute awe.

It wasn't a traditional bridal gown. It was a Collette Dinnigan creation that Catherine had bought—rashly almost emptying her bank account—to wear at the Academy Awards night, desperately wanting Zack to see her as the woman he always wanted at his side. She'd never worn it. The dress was the kind of dress that dreams were made of. It finally felt right to wear it today.

It was made of opalescent sequins, sleeveless, the

front bodice providing graceful movement with a long cowl neckline that dropped to below her waist, also showing quite a tantalising amount of cleavage. The slim-line style flared into a swinging skirt below the knees, allowing room to walk freely, though with a decidedly seductive swish.

'With your hair fluffed out over your shoulders and down your back, plus all those millions of glittering sequins, you kind of look like a mermaid, Catherine,' Livvy remarked assessingly, then laughed as she gestured to her own appearance. 'And I look like a whale.'

'No, you don't. You look absolutely beautiful, Livvy, and I'm sure Pete will tell you so.'

'Just as well you chose midnight-blue for me. It helps to minimise the lump.' She sighed. 'You could have waited another two months until after I'd had the baby. Having a matron of honour this pregnant is not fashionable.'

Catherine shook her head, smiling at the grumble. 'Babies are always fashionable, before and after they're born.'

'I can't see my feet anymore.'

'What's so great about your feet?'

'They're about the only part of me that hasn't swelled up. Which is just as well because I'll have you know I've done a lot of running around, getting this wedding right for you and Zack while you two did your jet-setting thing.'

'I know, Livvy.' Catherine kissed her cheek. 'Thank you so much for everything you've done for us.'

'Well it wasn't just me. Mum and Zack's mother were wild to get in on the act, very eager to get the two of you married. I'm sure Mum thought it was a miracle that you finally found someone.' Livvy raised a wagging finger. 'And she wasn't alone in that sentiment.'

Catherine grinned, recalling all her sister's match-making efforts. 'I didn't find Zack. It was a blind date, remember?'

Livvy rolled her eyes. 'And is Pete going to make capital out of that in his best man speech! He is so wrapped that we're all going to be connected by marriage. And so am I, Catherine.' She gave her a hug. 'It's great!'

'Yes, it is.'

With heartfelt pleasure beaming between them, Catherine couldn't keep the secret to herself any longer. It had to be safe now. The doctor had assured her all was well, and just this past week the scan had actually showed their baby sucking its thumb—so endearing it had brought tears to her eyes. Zack's, as well.

'We'll be sharing more than being in-laws, Livvy. I'm pregnant, too,' she happily announced.

'You're not!' It was a squeal of delight.

Catherine nodded.

Livvy clapped her hands. 'Oh, this is marvellous! How far along?'

'Almost four months.'

Sheer astonishment. 'You can't be! You're not even showing.' Her gaze dropped critically to Catherine's stomach.

'Luckily the long cowl on this dress hides a very definite mound.' She lifted it. 'See?'

Livvy pointedly examined the vital area. 'That's a very small four months. Trust you to keep nice and slim. I had a positive pot belly by then.' She frowned. 'How come you haven't told any of us before this?'

'I am older than you, as you've frequently mentioned,' Catherine answered carefully. 'I wanted to make it through the danger period first before letting anyone know there's a baby on the way.'

Livvy shook her head chidingly. 'You've got a very secretive nature. No doubt about it. We didn't even know you and Zack were an item until you announced your engagement. Honestly, Catherine, you could be a bit more forthcoming.'

'Oh, I don't know.' Her eyes were deliberately teasing. 'You do have a habit of telling me how to live my life, little sister.'

Livvy humphed and planted her hands challengingly on her hips. 'Well, Pete and I got it right putting you and Zack together, didn't we?'

Catherine laughed and hugged her. 'Yes, you did. Beautifully, wonderfully right.'

'The cars are here!' Their father yelled up the stairs. 'Are you girls ready?'

'Yes, Dad,' they chorused.

Livvy quickly pounced on the flowers she'd put on the bed. 'I'm glad I've got a bouquet to hold over my mountainous mound,' she declared. 'Why did you choose to carry just a single red rose, Catherine?'

She smiled, picking it out of the florist's box. 'It has its meaning.'

Livvy arched her eyebrows. 'I suppose that means you're not going to tell me.'

'Remember the red rose I wore in my hair as your bridesmaid?'

'Ah! You and Zack got together at *my* wedding!' Livvy cried triumphantly. 'Oh, I can't wait to tell Pete that!' She sailed off, smugly proud of having *fixed* her older sister's life for her.

Catherine lifted the perfect velvety bloom to smell its glorious scent. Not an artificial rose…a real one…as real as the love she and Zack had for each other.

The wedding guests were milling around the garden at Jonah's, the highly fashionable restaurant/reception centre Catherine and Zack had chosen, mostly because of its site on top of Sydney's northern peninsula, overlooking the ocean.

Everyone was clearly in a festive mood, enjoying the spectacular views as they waited for the bridal party to arrive. Zack and Pete stood closer to the clifftop above Whale Beach, watching the height of the waves rolling in as they'd done together hundreds of times throughout their long friendship.

'Not as good a surf as at Forresters,' Pete commented.

Zack smiled, remembering the night he and Catherine had shared at Spoon Bay. 'If a house comes up for sale close to yours, Pete, let me know.'

'Great idea!'

'Our kids could play together during vacations.'

'Yeah…' A cocked eyebrow. 'You and Catherine thinking of starting a family soon?'

Zack grinned. 'One already on the way.'

Pete punched his arm. 'You sly dog, you. Does your mother know?'

'Only just now. I whispered in her ear and her face lit up like a Christmas tree.'

'I can imagine. She's over the moon about your marrying Catherine.' Pete raised a scoring finger. 'And just you remember, I did tell you right from the start she was a knockout.'

'You did,' Zack happily conceded. 'And punctual.' He checked his watch. 'Five minutes to go. We'd better line up with the celebrant.'

He watched her come to him down the makeshift aisle, sunshine gleaming on her glorious hair, a light sea breeze rippling the long wavy tresses. Far below them the beat of the ocean on the sand echoed the beat of his heart, a rhythm that pounded to the name that swam in his mind.… Catherine… Catherine…

Her dress glittered like brilliant light on water. She seemed to flow towards him like some ethereal primeval goddess who would bestow upon him all the blessings of life. This was his wife to be, the woman who carried his child…the scan had revealed a boy…their son.

She smiled at him, her beautiful eyes glowing golden with love. He smiled back, knowing beyond any shadow of doubt this woman was utterly unique and irreplaceable, the one and only woman he would ever love. He saw she carried a single red rose and knew it represented her love for him—the giving and taking that was not a game, but an essential part of the marriage they both wanted.

He held out his hand to her. She slid hers over his palm and he closed his fingers around it.

Together, he thought.

It had felt right at the very beginning.

He knew it was right now, and would be so for the rest of their lives.

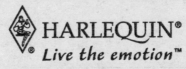

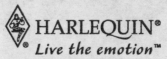

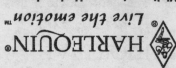

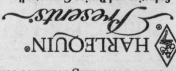

The world's bestselling romance series.

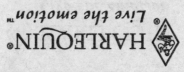

HARLEQUIN®

Presents®

Seduction and Passion Guaranteed!

GREEK TYCOONS

They're the men who have everything—
except a bride...

Wealth, power, charm—what else could a heart-
stopping handsome tycoon need? Find out in the
GREEK TYCOONS miniseries, where your very
favorite authors introduce gorgeous Greek
multimillionaires who are in need of wives!

Coming soon in Harlequin Presents®

SMOKESCREEN MARRIAGE by Sara Craven
#2320, on sale May 2003

THE GREEK TYCOON'S BRIDE by Helen Brooks
#2328, on sale June 2003

THE GREEK'S SECRET PASSION by Sharon Kendrick
#2339, on sale August 2003

Available wherever Harlequin books are sold.

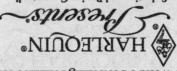

HARLEQUIN®

Live the emotion™